Now For Nola

Now for Nola

BY
LEE PRIESTLEY

Julian Messner
New York

Published simultaneously in the United States and Canada by
Julian Messner, a division of Simon & Schuster, Inc., 1 West
39 Street, New York, N.Y. 10018. All rights reserved.

For the blithe, brave young ones
who grow older and wiser.

Printed in the United States of America

ISBN 0–671–32317–2 Cloth Trade
0–671–32318–0 MCE

Library of Congress Catalog Card No. 70–123176

CONTENTS

Now For Nola

one ❦❦❦

WHAT'S FOR SURE?

Nola explained rapidly. Sometimes she could flood Pa with words until he would give in rather than listen. But it wouldn't work if he was angry; as he probably was now. She glanced at him, then looked away hastily.

"So there's no point in going on, Pa. Not with stuff that doesn't interest me one bit," she said airily.

Gerald Foret didn't answer immediately. Stretched in a wicker chair in the pleasantly cool courtyard, he seemed to remember the excellent lunch Louise, his wife, and Faimie, the cook, had produced. He watched drowsily as small Christy and Martin stalked silky-green tree frogs on the equally silken and green leaves of the banana plants.

But Julie Foret, younger than her sister Nola by two years and older by several in observation, saw the small straightening of Pa's mouth that meant clamping down on a rapidly slipping temper. Picking up the garden basket and shears, Julie began clipping the lemon thyme that grew between the flagstones, thus removing herself from the coming storm. Louise Foret, with the same idea, thought of a household matter requiring her presence inside.

Nola saw them go. She would get no help from the family . . . not that she expected to need it. Almost always she could bring Pa around to her way of thinking. Faimie called the procedure "winding that poor man around her finger."

So she went on confidently: "I could wait, I suppose, until end of term to drop out of the secretarial course. There's only a month to go—" She appeared to consider, although her mind was firmly made up. "But there's this fab part in the new play that Freddy Hefner absolutely certifies I can have. When I do it

10

well, there'll be no question about being accepted for
the fall term in drama school. I'm very excited about
it, Pa. This is it. Really it! I've never wanted to do anything so much."

Gerald Foret stirred in his chair. "Now when have
I heard that before?"

"How would I know, Pa? But tell me. What do
you think? About me changing over to the drama
school?"

Gerald Foret resumed his dreamy stare at the green
leaves tattered by weather and the children perching
the tiny frogs on their fingers. Julie, glancing at him,
clipped faster. Any minute now Pa would really ex-
plode.

Nola went on uneasily. Pa usually had a shorter
fuse. If he would go ahead and blow up, get it out
of his system, then she could get him to see things her
way, as usual.

"Wasn't I good in *An Honest Woman*, Pa? You said
so. Everyone did. Now Freddy Hefner thinks I can
have a real success—"

"I know what Hefner thinks. He pounced on me at
the club—clipped speech, pipe clenched in his teeth,
open shirt . . . the perfect picture of a director."

Nola saw Freddy in Pa's words, but this was no
time to agree with him. She overrode his interruption:
"Won't that be better than pounding a typewriter?
Oh, I know you don't have to pound an electric. This
part I can have in the comedy the theatre will do

11

next is really juicy. It's a real opportunity, Pa, really it is."

"I'm sure of that," Pa said mildly. "But so were all those other opportunities."

Nola frowned a little. What others? Sometimes Pa jumped right out of the conversation. "The thing is, I can't keep up the secretarial course and rehearse too. So I'll drop—"

The word galvanized Pa. He sat up abruptly. "You're seriously proposing another change?"

"You haven't been listening to me. It's making a change, yes. I want to drop the secretarial bit—I only started it to please *you*. It wasn't anything *I* wanted to do. You kept saying a girl should have some way to make a living if she needs to—"

"How are your grades this last period?"

Nola was indignant. "Have I ever had any trouble with grades?"

"Which makes it worse!" Pa was fierce now. "If you weren't blessed with brains and looks and the ability to do almost anything well, it wouldn't be quite so bad. For you, it all comes easy. You stand in the top ten percent of your class and hardly crack a book. You leap into something and in a few weeks flash past the plodders who have slaved for a year. I'll bet they'd love to wring your neck. Most of the time, like now, so would I!"

Christy and Martin left their frog catching to listen. Julie sat back on her heels, upsetting the basket and
12

spilling the lemon-scented cuttings into her lap. Mama had come to the doorway, and Faimie peered over her shoulder. The show deserved an audience.

Gerald, well launched, shook a finger under Nola's nose. "Look at you! Just look at you!" he commanded impossibly.

Nola was startled into trying. She could actually only see the tip of her pert nose. Pa saw her black hair cut short into a shining curly cap and her gray eyes. He saw, too, her sparkling and flushing with a temper that matched his own.

"You got a real head start," he shouted. "You're prettier and smarter, and more talented than half a dozen girls deserve to be! And what have you done with it all?" He ticked off on his fingers: "You've started out to be a musician, a model, a dancer, a painter. You've played with the notion of being an airline stewardess, a teacher, a nurse. But are you on the way to becoming any one of them? Not by a darn sight! You've had your successes, sure. You were great as a camp counselor, probably because camp didn't last long enough to bore you. Your mother's made you a good amateur interior decorator, and Faimie has taught you to cook. Outside of that, I've lost track of how often you've launched out on a great wave of enthusiasm and then paddled back to shore when the going got tough."

Nola sighed with exaggerated patience. "Pa, you've repeated all that so many times."

"You think it makes me happy that you don't listen to me? I don't know why I waste my breath. I know very well that the only time I could talk to my nineteen-year old was when she was ten!" Gerald's voice rose with his exasperation. "Whether you listen or not, daughter, you've dropped out for the last time. You are going to finish that secretarial course, if I have to lead you to class every day by your ear—*and* sit outside the door to keep you there."

Suddenly sure that Pa meant it, Nola protested: "How can you be so *mean!* Mama, are you going to let him do this to me? I *want* to go to drama school. My whole life will be ruined if I can't go!"

"All right!" Then Gerald stopped shouting as suddenly as he had begun. "Go to drama school"—he fixed Nola with a stern gaze that forbade any premature rejoicing—"*after* you've finished the secretarial course. Not a minute earlier."

"Pa, you're not being fair," Nola argued passionately. "I'll finish the blasted course some time. But now, you've got to let me do that play. I'll never have such a chance again. I have to go to drama school!"

Gerald nodded agreeably. "*After* you've finished this last term of your secretarial course. By the way, you'd better begin saving your allowance to pay your drama-school tuition."

Nola looked blank, then shocked. "I supposed . . . I thought—Pa, it's your duty to educate me!"

"I agree," Gerald said grimly. "That's all I'm trying

to do. I tell you what, dear. I'll find you a part-time job at the airline. Nothing so glamorous as a stewardness— you'd have to finish a school for that, and *we* know how you are about finishing anything. Maybe you can be a ticket clerk. If you hold down the job and save your pay, you can enroll in half a dozen drama schools with my blessing. *After* you finish that course."

"Oh, *you*! I won't—" Nola's rage nearly choked her.

In the silence Faimie was heard to say, "That changeable child found out somebody else can change some too."

In her room Nola threw herself on her bed and pounded a pillow with her fists. But that was silly, even in her frustration. She sat up as suddenly as she had cast herself down. Short of breaking the bottles on her dressing table or drumming the floor with her heels, she could think of nothing sufficiently violent to vent her anger.

How *could* Pa be so mean? Her reflection in the mirror mouthed the words again . . . *mean*! He hadn't seemed upset about things she had wanted to do before this. She had wanted to do many and various things, she admitted that. But Pa had encouraged her. He had taught her *himself* to swim and ride, to play tennis and golf, had insisted that she do everything well. Not that it had been a problem for her. They'd played chess every week until she could beat him sometimes, and Pa said her bridge game was sharp.

15

Pa treated Julie and Christy and Martin the same, but Mama sometimes sniffed about favorites. Faimie, with the privilege of an old friend, told Nola often that her Papa spoiled her scandalously. So how could Pa suddenly not want to spoil his favorite?

Julie poked her head in from the bath she shared with her sister. "First on the shower?"

"Why not? I'm probably confined to quarters, so time won't mean a thing to me. Who are you going out with?" Before Julie could reply, Nola answered her question herself: "Dix, of course. Julie, don't you ever want a change?"

"Depends," said Julie stepping out of her skirt. "What kind?"

"A different boyfriend. *Not* like Dix. Different stuff at school, not like those dreary rag-and-bone courses in archaeology you take."

"I like Dix," Julie said firmly. "And my courses aren't dreary. Not to me." She hung up her skirt and went into the bath.

She came back at once, stuffing her long hair under a shower cap. "I don't seem to feel the need to flit and flutter as you do." She looked curiously at her sister, now staring morosely into the branches of the tree outside the window. "Nola, what was all that with Papa? I mean, really? Why do you want to drop out of business ed? You wouldn't have to go that far to start something with Freddy Hefner. If you really wanted to, which I don't believe."

16

"I am sick—double sick!—of that secretary stuff, which I only started to please Pa. You know how he goes on: 'Maybe you won't marry, although being your mother's daughter I doubt it. But there are lots of ways to lose a husband and all sorts of situations in which you could find yourself needing to make your own living. So some place in your education you must'—"

The sisters finished the sentence in unison and a passable imitation of their father's voice: "—'acquire a skill that will enable you to get a job and hold it.'"

After they had laughed, Julie said, "He's right, you know."

"So he's right. I give him full leave to say, 'I told you so' when I have to take in washings. I get so *tired* of the parents trying to live my life for me."

"Lives," said Julie. "Plural. What upsets Pa is you trying to live more lives than Minette."

Hearing her name, the golden cat on the window seat stretched, then sprang upon the bed. Nola rubbed Minette's ears absently as she answered her sister.

"How can you not? I mean, what's for sure? With all the things to do in this world . . . all the places to go . . . all the people to meet! How can you be sure of what you want to do? How do you know when you want to settle for one place or one person?"

"I'll know," Julie said positively. "I'll know about me. It will seem right, that's all. But I don't know how you can know about *you*."

"A lot of help you are." But Nola grinned at her sister with affection.

Julie was looking at her speculatively. "What's this settling for one person? Nola, have you had a fight with Garry? There has to be an easier way to drop him than changing courses and having hysterics."

Nola shook her head. "That's not it. At least not all of it. I admit I'm tired of Garry. He's so tense. I liked him better when he was planning to take a real fine job with General Chemicals as soon as he graduated and saw his future all laid out before him—with me in it, naturally. He couldn't believe I didn't want to get married and for sure not to him. Then it occurred to him he might get drafted out of that real fine job, and bang! he's against the war and the government and especially General Chem." Nola thought about it. "I don't think I'd like getting shot at anymore than he does, but it seems to me he's playing both ends against the middle."

Julie had gone into the shower and shouted over the thrum and hiss of the water, "How do you mean?"

"Well . . . Like if you're going to take all the goodies the system provides—an education, a good job, all that—shouldn't you be willing to do your share to keep the system going? Anyway Garry's so busy justifying himself for going into grad school and staying safe at home that I can't stand him. So I did think if we didn't sit in the same classes and meet in the halls all day—"

18

"All that to brush him off? Why can't you just tell him?"

"He'll say I encouraged him."

"Well, didn't you? But after you break off with Garry, don't leap out of the frying pan into the foot-lights. Freddy Hefner is years too old for you and far too slippery."

Nola thought that was so. Freddy Hefner's interest was flattering, but she did understand it was no more than his line with a pretty girl who might enhance the cast of his play. No doubt he'd dazzled many a girl during his years as department head. Maybe she was learning even to question that expertise. "When it's just ourselves, darling, you may call me Freddy. When others are about, it might not sound sufficiently teacher-pupil." Had she thought that slightly ridicu-lous before now? Maybe Pa's maliciously accurate word picture of him had turned off the dazzle.

It could be that Pa was right about the secretarial course too, but Nola decided to die before she ad-mitted it to him. Julie said a thing "seemed right" to you—but what if a thing seemed right to you one day and wrong to you the next? She must be the change-able child Faimie muttered about.

A rat-a-tat on the wall outside her door was fol-lowed at once by Christy and Martin. "Hey, Sister," they said between them. "Papa sent us to tell you he's going to the airport in *two* minutes, and you'd better be ready to go with him."

19

Nola clutched her head and groaned. Pa was following through. He'd looked up her schedule and meant to get her to shorthand at three o'clock with time to spare. Going to the mirror, she began to comb her hair. She looked at her little brother and sister in the glass and blew a kiss to them.

"Tell Papa I'll be there, and he can have a minute back."

Martin said, "That's only sixty chimpanzees, Sister. You count, 'One chimpanzee' and that's one second."

"Here we go then." Nola began counting as she dealt with her hair. "One chimpanzee, two chimpanzees, three chimpanzees . . ."

Shutting off the shower, Julie heard the laughter and smiled. She shouldn't have worried. Nola couldn't stay disgruntled any more than she could hold a grudge.

"Atta girl!" Julie said around the bathroom door. "Heap sixty chimpanzees on poor Pa's head."

Laughing too, Nola winked and fitted her thumb and forefinger together in a small circle. Then she raced Christy and Martin to the stairs.

Louise and Gerald Foret were waiting at the courtyard gate, hand in hand. When they saw her coming, her father slung his jacket over his shoulder and bent to kiss his wife. Nola saw the look they exchanged. Their clinging fingers were a symbol of the married love that blessed the household. How marvelous to be so sure!

As he went off to bring the car around, Pa had a grin

for Nola that forgave her for the late altercation. Louise Foret kept her daughter at the gate with a detaining hand on her arm.

"You know Papa loves you and is only doing what he thinks is best for you."

Nola kissed her mother's cheek. "Don't worry, Precious. I'm not mad at Pa. I'm too lazy to stay mad at people. You and Pa know so exactly what you want, how come you had a daughter that swings like a weather vane? Oh, well . . . World-in-which-I-may-have-to-earn-my-living, here I come!"

two 🌸🌸🌸

"YOU BELIEVE IT WHEN IT HAPPENS TO YOU"

Sitting beside him Nola glanced at Pa, then looked away again. The set of his jaw, the tilt of his nose, the furrows in his forehead were uncompromising . . . strange and unfamiliar.

Her father didn't look away from the windshield

streaming from a sudden shower, but he had felt Nola's eyes on him. A smile took some of the grimness out of his face. "The old man surprised you, huh?" Before she could answer, he added, "Even surprised myself."

Nola slid over the seat to press close to his side. She laid her hand on his arm, her sigh of relief loud in her own ears. "Then you aren't mad at me, Pa?"

"Of course I'm mad at you. This grin is only a disguised snarl. It's possible to be furious and fond at the same time. I'm proving it."

"Oh, *you!* Pa, you're not going to make me finish that dreary old course!"

He reached out to pat her knee. "I am no longer twinable around the finger, daughter. Yes, you'll finish that dreary old course. At the top of the class too."

Nola couldn't see any give-in on his face or in his words. She punched his arm fiercely. "I don't mind the course so much, but I'm keen for a chance at that play, Pa!"

"If you're as good as Freddy Hefner thinks you are, he will find another good role for you."

Nola thought that was probably so. Although she wouldn't admit it to Pa, all those rehearsals were a drag. She got her lines and all the business after one or two times through a play, then had to stand around while the slower students learned their parts. Maybe she didn't want to be an actress. Maybe the grind outweighed the glamour.

23

"I'll have some time after classes," she began to plan.

Gerald shook his head. "Not so, dear. I meant all that about a job too. After your shorthand I'll be waiting out in the corridor to take you out to the terminal."

"I've got a choice?" Nola asked with resignation.

"No," Gerald said cheerfully. "There's a vacancy at the ticket desk. Or you could go into the air-freight office. The ticket wicket would suit you better, I should think."

Nola, being perverse, said, "No. I'll take the air-freight job."

"You'll be sorry. Frozen pheasants and tanks of live lobsters get heavy, and you won't always have someone to shift things when you need to see the labels. People send animals too, and the poor brutes get airsick."

"Never mind, I'm already sick enough," Nola said crossly.

After class, her father was true to his word. When the car pulled into the airport parking area, wet and shiny as licorice from the shower, Nola made no move to get out.

"I don't want to get splattered," she said. "Why can't you drive me over to the freight office?"

"No special privileges for you. You go through Personnel."

"That's silly. You own most of an airline. If you want to send your daughter to the salt mines, who's Personnel to say you can't?"

Pa laughed. "I don't anticipate any real trouble getting you hired, but there are some details. Run along now and fill in all the blanks."

Nola looked put upon, then ran through the cool, windy drizzle into the terminal. Having duly filled the blanks, she drew a set of uniforms and a desk assignment. A trim young woman at that desk looked up in curiosity.

"You mean you're going to work this spot?" she said. "Wonderful! I'm leaving to get married but I couldn't go until they found a replacement. I can surely use some time before the big day."

"Couldn't you just give notice and go?"

"Walk out without showing my replacement around? I couldn't do that. They've been good to me here, and what if I want to come back here to work some day? For now I'll go with my boy, but you never know about later."

Nola recited glibly the words she had heard so often: "There are lots of ways to lose a husband and all sorts of situations in which you could find yourself needing to make your own living."

"You sound as if you're quoting. It's the truth, whoever said it."

"My father. Look, should you show me things? Forms and paper clips and what to do before the boss comes?"

The girl was efficient. "Now here. Type these in triplicate—you couldn't do them any other way, because they're set up with the carbons. Bills are done like this, and you file like this—"

After a time Nola understood what would be expected of her. She smiled at the other girl. "I think I have it."

"You're awfully quick. I won't have a chance to get this desk back if I need it, except that you're too good looking not to marry and leave. What's your name?"

"Nola Foret." She waited for the surprise.

The girl pointed a finger at her. "The boss's daughter?"

Nola nodded. "As I told you, I have to acquire a skill that will enable me to hold a job because I might not marry, and if I do—"

"—there are lots of ways to lose a husband!"

They were laughing together when Gerald came for Nola. As she went with him to the parking area, watching the carts and loaders darting through the glimmering splotches of reflected neon or skating like water bugs over the wet mirror of the pavement, Nola found her spirits lifting. All the hum and hustle of people and planes—it wouldn't be such a drag after all. But she wouldn't admit it to Pa.

A week later, Nola's spirits were still high. The glow even spread to the despised secretarial classes. She liked her job. Not even a wretchedly airsick Great Dane daunted her. It was provoking, but Pa had been right.

26

She was sorting forms one day when a shadow fell across her desk. Lifting her eyes for a long moment, she couldn't believe what they told her. Why was the air full of sparks?

He was tall and tanned and too thin. Sun-streaked hair, brown eyes flecked with green, a strong chin and an amused mouth. . . . His uniform and his captain's bars looked shiny new, but he had a jaunty assurance that matched his winged insignia. Without taking her eyes from his face, Nola accepted a paper from strong fingers faintly grimy and smelling of machinist's soap.

He was staring too. Nola felt a warm flood of color rising in her face. Annoyed with herself for being so naïve, she turned rosier then ever.

The young officer said, "Don't mind. I'm losing my cool, too!" He touched Nola's cheek carefully with a forefinger. "You are real. I was afraid I was day-dreaming."

Captivating was the word for the captain. Nola had trouble keeping her mind on the business that had brought Tom Cartright to her desk—and thanked Heaven that it had!

He asked about a missing set of plates, not everyday metal but an exotic amalgam or alloy light in weight with fiber glass and plastic foam sandwiched between and to be used for helicopter shielding. Nola didn't really understand.

She was watching the ways of his mouth, at once shy and assured, or the lift of an eyebrow when he

27

stared at her, and forgot what he was saying. But he wanted to tell her all about it.

Those plastic plates were overdue. Consequently, his work on the development of better shielding for helicopters was being held up. On detached duty from the Air Force, he was putting together a prototype shield. In Vietnam, where the choppers worked normally under fire as they supported or relieved ground troops, all the shielding possible was needed. "When you have to hover over a veritable barrage, believe *me* you need a whole suit of armor!"

His experimental unit depended entirely upon the choppers. They flew all kinds, from miniscouts to giant cranes to rocket-shooting gun ships, under battle conditions to test experimental tactics. "You can understand," he said, "how vital it is to shield the choppers from heavy machine-gun fire. Enemy guns, dug in and well camouflaged, can deliver a deadly fire up to five thousand feet. One such gun in a landing zone could bring down troop carriers like flies off a ceiling."

Nola shivered. "Troops" had been an impersonal word until now. Violence on the other side of the world in a tragic war hadn't really touched her. She hadn't joined any of the demonstrations against the war, but that was more because of a distaste for many of the demonstrators and their methods than out of conviction. She didn't know what she thought about the moral rightness or wrongness of the conflict, but with an empathy that knifed through her heart she

28

shared the anguish of thousands of girls to whom thousands of men at war were the center of their lives—as was this man who had become the most important thing in the world to her. She must listen to what he was saying—

"In a heliborne assault, the landing zone must be carefully studied by aerial reconnaissance," he explained. "We use small scout choppers that often fly below treetop level and as slowly as ten miles an hour. That way they can spot the traps. So you see why we need the best shielding we can get? The 'slicks' filled with troops don't have heavy armament, and the rescue choppers and the ones that take out the wounded need protection too—"

That word again. But "troops" wasn't an impersonal word now. It meant men like this one to girls like Nola Foret.

He had spread his hands in a gesture that asked, "You see?" "Even the choppers bringing in hot chow don't need the main course ventilated. And when they bring up the mail, it's bad for morale to have the tender messages from your best girl shot out of your letters." He grinned a little. "That hasn't been my problem."

"No missing messages in your mail?"

"No best girl to write me."

So the captain needed those plastics for R, D and T. (Nola worked that out after a moment: Research, Development and Testing.) The sooner he could get

29

the proto together, the sooner it could be tested under combat conditions. He stopped talking then and stood looking at her. Finally he remembered to ask, "So where are those plates?"

Nola didn't know, but she knew where to begin looking. When the tracer was well started, he murmured to her bent head, "I'll wait for you in the lounge."

"I'm not off for an hour."

"I'll still wait."

Nola watched his erect, well-drilled back going away. He had taken it for granted that she would meet him. And she would. At the door Tom hung back a moment, his gaze speaking to her across the intervening space.

Nola knew with a shiver that ran from her head to her toes what had happened. Love. The unbelievable lightning had struck them both.

"You have to believe it when it happens to you," Nola thought.

In the coffee shop they sat while their cups cooled untasted. At first they didn't talk much. They looked at each other. When they started again on another cup, they found words for their mutual astonishment.

"It's as if I'd known you all my life," Nola marveled.

"Without knowing a thing about you, I know you better than I know myself," Tom said.

He looked down at her hand in her lap, then covered it with his own. After a moment her fingers turned

30

and curled confidingly into his clasp. They smiled at each other, amused by those knowledgeable hands.

"There are a few unimportant things I should know about," Tom said. "Like, are you married? I don't see any rings."

Nola hooted. "Would I be acting like this if I were?"

As they talked, Nola felt she was babbling, but Tom seemed to like it. So she kept talking. They began to find out things about each other. For one, Tom was six years older. For two, he was a career man. He had come out of the academy with an engineering degree and had served three years on active duty, some of that just behind him in Vietnam. He was working on the helicopter modification in the shops at the air base, so he would be around for a while at least—especially if those plates didn't turn up.

"Then I hope they can't be—"

Tom was shaking his head, his dark eyes intent on her words.

Nola understood. "I don't mean that!" To delay the shielding would bring death or danger to those other men who were the center of the world to other girls. She resolutely put the thought of war out of her mind.

"I don't understand us," she said. "You and I."

"The way it hit us? How did you think it would be?"

"Not like a head-on collision with a stranger!"

"Am I a stranger?"

"That's what frightens me. Why aren't you?"

31

"When I stood in that doorway, feeling the letdown of a strange place, I saw you and came home. I knew I'd found the girl I want to marry. So how can I be a stranger to you?"

"*Marry!*" The word shocked Nola. "I don't even know your middle name!"

"Thomas Allan." He grinned a little. "Anything else?"

For the next several hours they concentrated on those things. . . .

"For the Lord's sake, Nola!" Gerald Foret said grimly. "Your mother's out of her mind! I've been phoning hospitals for the past hour."

She stared at Pa unseeingly for a moment, her hand tightening in Tom's as he rose to his feet beside her. She shook her head a little, blinking at the angry face above. It was Pa, but why was he so mad?

Only then did she notice that lights were on in the coffee shop. The wide windows giving on the field were dark mirrors reflecting Pa's anger and the sidewise smirk of a passing waitress. She and Tom must have sat here for hours.

"I called the agent out of a meeting," Pa was saying, "but all he knew was that you had gone at the usual time. Louise and Julie called every living soul who knows you. I even checked the morgue. Then we found your car in the parking area—" Pa ran out of breath and self-control at the same time. "Who the devil are you?"

Nola wanted to laugh but thought better of it. Pa was too furious. Before Tom could answer, Gerald turned on Nola. "I'll take care of you later, young woman! Frightening your mother like this! Don't you stir until I phone Louise. Then I want to hear an explanation. And it better be good!"

When he had whirled off, Nola did laugh, but she grew serious again quickly. "Why didn't we see how late it was getting? It will be hard enough to tell Mama and Pa I've found the man I mant to marry without them thinking you're a kidnapper."

"What?" Tom looked surprised. "Did we talk about getting married? Not right now. Sometime soon, sure—"

Nola's glare was a feminine version of her father's. "Tom Cartright, you said we'd be married the first chance we got!"

Tom hastily took her hands. "I meant every word I said. Whatever they were. But you're such a kid and there's a war on. When a girl marries into the service, she's got to give it a good think—"

"All the more reason for not waiting. How do we know how much time we have to be together? Oh, Tom . . ."

When Gerald Foret came back, they had gone off into a private world of their own.

Gerald put them both into his car. "You're in no condition to be trusted in traffic," he had growled at Tom. "How you and Nola get your cars back to wherever you want them is no concern of mine."

Driving, he spoke to Tom over Nola's head as she sat meek and silent between them. "She's never done anything like this before." Ignoring their quiet, he went on, "Now kindly shut up, the both of you, until I get you home to Louise. Maybe she can make some sense out of you."

The family was in the living room when they came in: Louise white-faced, her dark eyes glittering with unshed tears, her mouth tight to forestall its trembling; Julie an animated question; Christy and Martin big-eyed, and Faimie in the hall distracted and muttering. Nola ran to her mother, pouring out an incoherent mixture of regrets for having distressed her and excuses for her absence.

"Mama, I'm so truly sorry—Mama, here's Tom." She held out a hand to draw him closer. "I wouldn't have caused all this worry purposely, but we got to talking, and the time just went, that's all."

Julie shook her head in unbelief. "You sat in the coffee shop at the airport all the time we were searching the town for you? You forgot a date with Freddy Hefner too. Don't count on any preferred treatment from him now. He stood around for half an hour, then went off puffing out a smoke screen of disapproval."

"Yes, we did—" Nola stared at the clock with her

mouth a little ajar. "That can't be right. Tom, we sat there for five hours!"

"You didn't get up even once?" Christy asked with interest.

"Not even to go to the bathroom?" said Martin.

It was Tom who answered the little boy: "Not even once. And we drank gallons of coffee. Would you like to show me the way?"

"It's closest down the hall," said Martin.

They looked after the tall soldier blandly following the little boy. Suddenly Nola ran out of the room too and upstairs, with Julie at her heels.

The ones who were left began to laugh, half-hysterical with relief.

three 🦋🦋🦋

"WAIT" IS A LONELY WORD

Gerald Foret and Tom stood in the hall talking quietly. Mama and Faimie and the two small ones were gone, bedtime being long past.

"Come on, girls," Gerald beckoned when Nola and Julie came downstairs again. "I'll drive us all back to the airport so Captain Cartright can get his car. Then Julie can ride home with you, Nola, and I'll follow you back."

"Why don't I call a taxi?" Tom asked.

"You could, but that wouldn't get Nola's car home." Gerald waved a hand, dismissing any more protests. "I know. I said how you got your transport straightened out was no concern of mine, but I've had second thoughts. Why risk losing a tire or a battery just to be spiteful?"

On the street Gerald put Tom in the front seat of his car. "You and Nola can't have a word left for each other," he said. "The sisters can sit in back."

"I don't think I do have any conversation left," Nola said to Julie. "Why does Pa always have to be right?"

"What did you talk about all that long?"

"Oh, things." Nola was vague.

In the front seat Gerald was getting more definite information. Tom came from a small town in the Southwest, or more specifically, from a ranch near that small town. His father was a retired Army officer with a slight, service-incurred disability, now happily raising cattle and horses. Tom's mother had inherited the land and contributed ranching known-how from her childhood to the family partnership.

"No," said Tom, "I'm not much of a rancher. I found my career in the Air Force. I'm a professional soldier." There was pride in his voice.

Hearing that, Julie whispered to Nola, "Do you

want to marry an officer? It's the last thing I ever thought you'd do."

Nola whispered back, "I just want to marry Tom."

"Same thing."

"Maybe not." It didn't have to be that way, Nola thought with a rising excitement. She couldn't let Tom risk the life that was already so precious to her. When they were married, she would persuade him to resign. The world was full of jobs for an engineer . . . jobs he would like and be just as proud to do.

Now Pa heard about the overdue plastics and the plan to combine them with fiber glass as a shielding for the helicopters. "That's what you're doing in the shops out at Air Defense? How far along is your modification?"

"If that shipment comes in . . . two weeks more should see the proto finished," Tom said.

"And then?"

"Testing under field conditions."

"For which read 'Vietnam'," Pa said.

The two men were silent then. Nola felt the sympathetic clasp of Julie's hand and tried to swallow the panic rising in her throat. She knew, helplessly, that she couldn't keep Tom from going back . . . not this time. But three years of fighting was enough. When, pray God, he came home safely, he must not return to danger. He had done his share; let someone else take his place—

38

As they turned into the parking area, Pa said to Tom, "Louise hopes you will come to dinner tomorrow. Check with Nola. Good night now, Captain."

Julie took the key from Nola and walked ahead to the the car. Tom caught Nola's hand and drew her close to his side. They walked together as the beams from Gerald's turning car laid a pathway of golden light for their feet.

"For only a little while," Tom said softly as he handed her into the car.

Nola's hand clung to his, reluctant at parting for even so short a time.

As Tom went away to his own car, the sisters followed their father out of the parking area. Nothing was said for several blocks. Then Nola asked, without much curiosity, "Why are you driving my car?"

"I wondered when you'd notice. We couldn't sit waiting until you surfaced out of your sea of dreams. Neither did I want to ride with *you* driving. Not fogged in as you are."

"It isn't like a fog," Nola said seriously. "It's more like . . . like being inside the sunlight. Warm . . . bright . . . comforting."

Julie shook her head. "I've never seen you in such a state before."

"I've never been in such a state before either. Remember what I asked you this afternoon how I'd know when I wanted to settle down with one person? I still

39

don't know *how*, but I have. And don't tell me I'll feel different in a week, or a month or a year! I won't. This is for true."

Nola shivered a little as their motion stirred up a breeze that cooled her flushed face. Was the shiver as much thoughtful as thermal? For a tiny doubt had crept into her mind. How could she be so sure?

Next morning Nola woke to a world bright with promise, hushed in anticipation. The marvel of this sunny day would be Tom. Grateful that they had come together, just two out of billions, Nola said her morning prayers over again. It was old-fashioned to believe that if you waited—with all the due circumspection advised by mothers and deans of women—Mr. Right would come along. But you had to believe it when so obviously right a Mr. Right actually came!

She daydreamed through her classes, then in the afternoon hurried to her car, her thoughts winging ahead to her desk in the cargo section at the terminal. Anytime after she got there Tom would come through that door again. . . .

But Garry Somers caught her before she could drive away. Leaning in the door, he reached across to snap off the ignition. "I get the idea you're avoiding me lately."

"Don't be stupid, Garry. But, honestly, I have to go to work."

"That's new. Since when are you so anxious to get to a job your Pa made you take?"

Mama was right, Nola thought. Mama said anytime you talked about family matters to an outsider, you'd regret it. Nola shouldn't have told Garry that Pa had made her take the job. Or Freddy Hefner either.

"Because Papa *said*. He doesn't put his foot down so often I can ignore it when he does."

"Do you have to knock yourself out? Any day now they'll award you an 'E' flag, recognizing all your effort." He stared at her consideringly. "Who's the new man in it?"

Nola bent over the steering wheel, dropping her face into her hands in an overdone gesture of exasperation she hoped would hide the flush she felt rising. "I *told* you. I'm going to enter drama school. So I have to talk things over with Freddy Hefner, don't I?"

"Your neck has turned the exact color of boiled shrimp," Garry observed. "I'm not talking about God's-gift-to-silly-girls Freddy. It has to be somebody out at the terminal," he guessed. He opened the door and slid into the seat beside Nola. "Thanks, yes. I will ride out with you. And get a look at my competition."

"Garry Somers, get out of my car! Or I'll . . . I'll . . ."

"Nola—" The half-angry teasing had gone out of Garry's voice. He repeated her name. "Nola, you really meant it, then."

41

She could think of nothing that would erase the misery in his face. "Garry, we were just friends. If I ever led you to believe it was more than that—"

He shook his head. "You didn't. I just couldn't see how you could resist old irrestistible me, if you were exposed to my charms long enough."

"You aren't in love with me."

"I'm not? It sure feels like it."

"No, you're not. One day you'll really fall in love with some lucky girl, not a changeable chick like me who doesn't know her mind three days running." But she did know her mind now, Nola thought. You knew. It was as simple as that. Tom. "We are good friends, Garry. We've had fun going around together, but we knew that's all it was. Isn't that right?"

"No, not about me. I knew you weren't serious, but you know that fellow who said, 'One loves and one is beloved.' So I hoped—" He stared into her face, suddenly intent. "You wouldn't fire up like this over ole Phoney Freddy, would you?"

"Not him. It's a man I met—" She stopped herself from adding, "yesterday."

"Does he live here? Where did you meet him? At the terminal?"

"No, he doesn't live here. He came into the office looking for a shipment of plastic and fiber glass. He's developing a helicopter shield. For use in Vietnam."

"A soldier?" There was horror in Garry's voice. "My

42

Lord, Nola! I didn't think you'd fall for a uniform. What is he, one of these citizen-soldiers?"

"No, he's a career man," Nola said reluctantly.

"That's worse. One of the blood-and-glory boys, huh? Just because it's wartime, everything in uniform isn't hero stuff," Garry said darkly. "What about your mother and father? They surely won't let you get in deep with some two-legged stranger."

"They couldn't agree with you more."

"Do you know anything about him? You have to watch it, honey. This love-at-first-sight is tricky. Anyway, what's your hurry? Why not take a good look?"

Nola laughed a little. "I have, Garry. Honestly."

Garry wasn't mortally wounded, she felt sure. When they were seniors in high, Dottie Broussard had been the one and only for him. Then there was Marcia Somebody, and Sue Myers— If she gave a dinner party to show Tom off to her friends, she could pair Garry with Sue, who was in a break-off cycle herself just now. Garry would heal fast.

"Now, will you get out of my car, *please*?" she asked. "I'll be late."

"Look, Nola. Is it because I decided to stay in grad school instead of volunteering, all noble like? I'm not doing any more or less than I'm entitled to. A man has to think of his future."

Anger flashed in Nola's mind. What about the men who weren't in graduate school, who didn't have the brain or the opportunity to find a draft haven. What about their futures? Then the anger went away again. She couldn't scorn Garry when all she wanted in the world was just such a safe spot for Tom.

She shook her head. "No, it isn't that at all. *Please*, Garry. I'll be awfully late."

"Okay, I'll go quietly." He opened the car door, then turned to pull her into his arms. "It was nice. Very nice while it lasted. If you ever change your mind—" He interrupted himself to kiss her, lightly at first. When she pushed him away, he got out, slammed the door and walked away without looking back.

Nola watched him go for a moment. It had been nice. She had liked Garry . . . as she had liked other boys. They had all talked of love, but "like" was all they meant. Or, at least, all she had meant. When you knew the difference, as she did now, the gulf between like and love was all the greater.

She trod on the starter, her thoughts already across town with Tom.

She was aware of him the moment he came. As she straightened from a file cabinet, her gaze flew to the door at the end of the long room. There he was. Their eyes met, and as he walked toward her, Nola's heart tried to go to him.

When he stood beside her desk, she subsided weakly in her chair. "Hello."

"Hi, honey. I've got news. Those plates came in, and they fit like a charm." His voice was bright with success. "That proto will be ready in about half the estimated time."

Nola tried, but her voice sounded dead to her own ears. "Then you'll go back."

He nodded. "That shielding is badly needed." He rubbed his eyes, which were red and tired. "The work is going real fine. I stayed with it through two shifts."

"Didn't you go to bed at all?"

"I couldn't chance someone goofing up a plate. It would take too long to replace. This has been my baby all the way, so I don't want to leave it now. Rewarding to see an idea turn into armor."

The eyes that were red were also bright with enthusiasm. Nola felt a twinge that could only be jealousy. Could you be jealous of plates and presses and an intent machinist? Of course.

She could be jealous of anything and everything that took Tom's full attention away from herself. She wasn't exactly proud of the feeling, but there it was. What a poor time to recall what Garry had said—that one loves and one is beloved. What if Tom didn't love her as much as she loved him? Suddenly she saw Garry's stiff back, walking away from her. Understanding how he felt was the thing called empathy.

"I wanted to be here when you came," Tom was saying. "Then I'll catch a nap and be back to pick you up when your trick is over. Four thirty, isn't it? I wouldn't like your mother to see me looking as if I'd had a night on the town."

Nola had forgotten that Mama had asked Tom to come to dinner. She didn't want to share him with the family. Not with anyone. They needed to be with each other.

Tom glanced quickly around the room. The girls at the other desks were intent on papers or opening file drawers or walking away. He kissed Nola swiftly. "In the snack bar at quitting time," he said, and went away.

Nola sat, lost in the whirl of her emotion. The other girls looked up from their papers, closed the file drawers, came and went past her desk. They spoke to her, and she must have made the proper answers for they didn't look astonished. After a time she too examined papers, filed them in the correct places and collected others. But she could not have told what she did, only that her heart hammered over and over, "Sure . . . sure . . . sure . . . sure."

It seemed years before she could finish her work, clear her desk and home in on the snack bar. Tom waited for her there and, laughing, turned her away from the table.

"After yesterday, maybe we shouldn't sit down over coffee. Anyway, it's more private in the parking area."

When he had put her into his car and gone around to slide under the wheel, she turned into his arms without a word. Held tight against his chest, Nola felt

46

Tom's heart beating with her own. After a moment she lifted her face to him.

Nola looked past the flowers Julie had arranged with care, marking the importance of the occasion. Dinner was a great success. The food had been perfect and Tom—well, he had been charming with Mama, amusing with Julie and delightful with Christy and Martin. Now he was man-to-man-ing with Pa about the helicopter shielding.

Nola prickled with a silly jealousy. He had scarcely talked to her. It must have been some silly girl, head-over-heels, of course—like Nola Foret—who had said, "All for love and the world well lost." Men didn't think like that. She thought about feeling neglected.

When they were married, she would have Tom all to herself. Wasn't that what marriage was all about? To permit two people to live together in a private world. There was that part in the service about "forsaking all others, keep thee only unto him." Nola had gone to enough weddings to remember that. Some of her friends had married after high school; even more left college with wedding bells pealing. The married didn't as a rule see much of their single friends, so the "forsaking all others" must mean the old crowd and perhaps even the family.

Nola saw Mama watching her as she watched Tom. Mama's smile was understanding, perhaps a little wryly amused, even a little sad.

47

"Men are different, that's all," Mama said to her softly under the cover of the men's talk about angle of penetration and a sandwich of plastic with a filling of fiber glass. "No matter how much they love you, don't believe you are all in all to them. I'm afraid you aren't old enough to accept that, dear. It takes maturity to love a man for what he is, not for the changes you hope to make in him."

Nola hadn't really listened, so she smiled at Mama and did not answer. Mama wanted to be helpful, Nola supposed, but how could she know what was right for them? Tom and Nola were unique; their love was unique too.

She looked at Christy across the table. "What did you say, dear?"

"I didn't say. It was Martin."

"I asked you where your car is, Sister," Martin said. "When I went to put my bicycle in the garage, it wasn't there."

At the end of the table, Pa heard and groaned. "Don't tell me, Nola. You've left your car in the parking at the terminal again. You and Tom will have to work it out tonight yourselves. You're younger, and I'm too tired to cross town two more times tonight."

Nola looked at him reproachfully. Pa didn't need to read her mind. Neither did he need to take her thoughts about "forsaking all others" so literally. He shouldn't abandon her and Tom until they got the cars sorted out, anyway.

48

four 💗💗💗
PRIVATE WORLD

A week later the sisters freshened hair and makeup in the ladies' lounge at the air terminal before meeting Tom in the snack bar. Nola met Julie's eyes in the mirror.

"Go on. Say it!"

49

"I will. I'm surprised at you. This isn't like you. Not one bit."

Nola brushed her hair forward. Shaking it back and pressing it into a crisp cap, she agreed with Julie. This wasn't like her. Maybe she was out of her mind. Mama halfway thought so, and was almost ready to lock her oldest daughter in her room until she came to her senses. And Pa agreed with Mama.

Nola fitted a last lock into place. "Why should all of you jump on me," she complained, "just because I fell in love at first sight? Plenty of people do. Mama and Pa did."

Julie's amazement grew to horror. "Love? Nola, you can't believe you've fallen in love? With a complete stranger?"

"Tom isn't a stranger," Nola said impatiently. How many times had she repeated that in the past few days! "Pa's checked Tom forward and backward, and I know him better than most of the people I've grown up with." She swung around on the dressing-table bench and took up her bag. "But I'm sick to death of arguing about it. Let's go, or Tom will think we've run out on him."

"We could," said Julie hopefully. "There's a side door, and we could call a taxi." She caught Nola's arm. "Before you go any further, Sister, are you *sure*?"

Nola fisted her sister's chin, lightly flipped the end of Julie's pert nose. "You can stop worrying about that. Yes, I'm sure. Really, truly sure."

Tom was watching the doorway. When their eyes met aross the crowded snack bar, the welcoming gladness in his face was reflected, Nola knew, in her own. Whoever loved most, the attraction was mutual. Tom felt it as surely as she did.

He took her hands, the cling of their fingers as real a caress as the meeting of their eyes had been. Sight and touch transported them into the private world they had found in each other.

Julie made an impatient clucking noise. When they looked questioningly at her, the impatience was in her words: "You aren't the only people on earth. Let's go sit down. To stand here with you two drowning in each other's eyes is a bit conspicuous."

When they found chairs at a corner table overlooking the runways, Julie sighed and fell silent. Was this jealousy she felt, or envy? The sister she loved dearly bore little resemblance to this starry-eyed stranger. So the painful twinge, the sense of loss could be jealousy of this man who was suddenly the most important person in Nola's life. Julie herself had never fallen in love to the extent of starry eyes and a private world, so perhaps she envied Tom and Nola.

She had emptied her coffee cup before theirs were more than touched. Finally Julie rapped lightly on the table with an air of bringing the meeting to order. Again she shook her head at their questioning gaze, feeling years older than her seniors.

"You *did* have some reason for bringing me here on

51

a busy afternoon?" She looked from Tom's uncomprehending face to Nola's, which had grown carefully innocent. "Give, sweetie," she said to her sister. "What do you have up your sleeve? I can see Tom knows nothing about it."

Now that it was time to tell, Nola drew back, figuratively, from the brink. She should have talked to Tom first. And alone. But she had known what he would say. That was the reason for bringing Julie. In front of Julie, Tom would surely find it hard to refuse.

The two of them stared at her, waiting. The words came hard. She knew how Tom felt about her. She knew how she felt about him. They were in perfect agreement about wanting to be married. Why then should she hesitate to voice the plan that would let them be together long before the stuffy ideas of her parents would permit? Perhaps she was usurping Tom's prerogative? She hastily denied that to herself.

So she blurted out what she could not find a graceful way to say: "Tom, I want us to get married right now! That's why I brought Julie along. Because we'll need her help. Mama and Pa think we shouldn't get married until you get back from Vietnam, and I can't *stand* it, Tom! I can't bear it! To have you go away to that awful place! So I've decided I won't wait. I know you don't want to wait to be married either. We don't know how much time we have together, and I don't want to lose a single minute of it. Say you don't either!"

52

It wasn't so much that she had run out of breath. The two astonished, even shocked, faces in front of her dammed her flooding words.

"Nola, how could you!"

"Honey, do you know what you're saying?"

She caught her breath again and found more words: "I can, because I must. And I do too know what I'm saying. I won't let you go away without marrying me, Tom. I mean it!"

Julie pushed her chair back. "You don't need me now. Tom, I wouldn't have come if I'd had the least idea, so I'm going home again."

"Julie, don't go!" Nola's voice was a wail.

But Tom nodded as he got to his feet. "I'll see you later, Sister-in-law." With a not too gentle hand under her arm, he stood Nola up, too. "We'll go sit in my car. Nola and I have a few things to talk over and a spot of privacy is indicated."

Nola came along as meekly and wordlessly as a child sent to the principal's office, Julie thought with a suppressed grin. But the amusement went away in a wave of annoyance with her sister. Nola was smarter than this. She left them with a wave of her hand, but she saw out of the corner of her eye that in Tom's car Nola had flung herself into his arms—and not been repulsed. They would work it out because they did love each other.

They sat quietly after Nola had stopped her stormy weeping. At last she moved, accepting his handkerchief to mop her eyes, sniffing childishly. "Blow," said Tom. She blew obediently.

After another time they faced each other and spoke together:

"Tom—"

"Nola—"

They started again.

"I'm sorry—"

Tom laughed a little. "This must mean we are both anxious to meet the other halfway. Look, Nola. Let's go on as if the last half hour never happened."

She lifted her chin stubbornly. "No, Tom. We must talk it out. Or it will nag away at us like . . . like a stomachache," she finished inelegantly. "I meant all I said, Tom. I meant it, because I love you and can't bear the thought of being separated from you."

"I love you too, little crackpot," Tom said tenderly. "But you can't go with me to Vietnam."

"I know that. If we could be together, even for a few days, I'd feel surer that you'd come back to me."

"No, that would only make it harder. Anyway you might let me do my own proposing."

"I know I was wrong to blurt it out the way I did," Nola said contritely. "How else could you know that I was prepared—*am* prepared—to go against my parent's wishes and be married now?"

"I know all right. For instance, I don't think you kiss the men you go out with"—he stopped to lift her chin in his hand—"like this."

Shaken by the kiss, Nola leaned in the circle of his

arms until her heart stopped pounding. Then she said in a small voice, "You don't think we should? Get married, I mean?"

"I do not. I have to go back in another week. You know that."

He kissed her quickly, then moved her to the far side of the seat. "Sit over there and stop distracting me until I forget what I want to say next. Look, now. I won't be gone long this time. We'll check out the shield under field conditions, and then I may have something to do with getting it into production. So you use this time to be sure—" He waved a hand to stop Nola's protests. "I won't change, but I've seen a lot of girls. I don't intend to rush into marriage with a kid that may write me a Dear John letter in six months. I know, I know. *You* won't. So next week you kiss me good-bye and start deciding which color garbage disposal you want and how many bridesmaids to have. Or whatever girls do when they get serious. I want you to stay serious. See?"

Nola sighed. "Why won't you believe I can stay in love?"

"Because you're such a kid. You've still got peanut butter and jelly on your face. How do you know you're ready to be a wife?"

For a humble moment, Nola doubted that she did know.

The hours alternately flew when she was with Tom or stretched into deadly eternities when she was not.

55

If Tom had been free during class time, Nola would have defied Pa and cut every session. Since the time had to be gotten through until he could leave the shops out at the base, she might as well be marked present. But she was only alive during the hours she spent with Tom.

Mama looked pitying; Pa mostly looked provoked. Faimie muttered about "wooly-headed younguns"; Julie waved a hand in front of Nola's face when they met in the hall and advised her to wake up.

Nola did wake up . . . when she was with Tom. Together they sat in front of food they forgot to eat, went to movies they didn't see, walked for miles and couldn't remember where they had been, said endlessly the fond and foolish nothings that make up the vocabulary of love. Neither of them mentioned the parting that rushed toward them, but it loomed constantly at the back of Nola's mind. She knew it haunted Tom as well.

The last day came, its precious time to be together compressed into a few minutes before dinner and a few hours after. Tom came to the house, having decided that Nola couldn't see him off at the airport at three o'clock in the morning. Determinedly casual, they ate Faimie's court bouillon, all day in the making, without tasting it. They talked brightly but scarcely noticed when the family stopped listening and propelled them into the courtyard before taking themselves off.

In the old wicker swing, Nola's head on Tom's shoulder and his arm holding her close to his side, they watched without much talk as the moon path reached slowly into the garden and the minutes slipped away. The cool silvery light crossed the slates, bleaching the ruffs of the lemon thyme to a ghostly gray and picking out gleaming highlights on the silken tatters of the banana plants. Insect hum and twing and the murmur of water in the pool made only enough sound to measure the silence against.

"It isn't as if I'm going to the end of the world," Tom said once. "In six weeks I'll come back to Hawaii to do some work there."

" 'Only!' "

"What if I were going to the moon?"

"I wouldn't let you," Nola said fiercely. "How can the wives of the astronauts stand it!"

"They know about their husband's work when they marry," Tom said reasonably. "As you know about mine."

"I may not let you go to Vietnam either." Nola turned in his arms. "Oh, Tom, why can't you run off to Canada? Or burn up your draft card!"

Tom made a small amused sound. "Sweetie, I'm a soldier. A soldier goes where the war is. And a soldier's wife kisses him good-bye and sends him off with a smile. . . . Or so I've been told."

"Don't look for any smiles from me. Besides, I'm not a soldier's wife and you-know-who kept me from being! Don't expect me to act like a brave big girl. I'm not and I won't."

She clung to him fiercely. He rallied her with more carefully casual talk—at one point he was telling her about some of the Army wives whom she promptly hated as paragons with stiff upper lips—but his kisses matched the desperation with which she returned them.

When the hour inexorably arrived, she managed to send him away with something resembling a smile, wobbly and damp around the edges as it was. Standing at the gate, Tom's last kiss warm on her mouth, she watched his car turn the corner with a wink of brake lights as a last message. And Nola made up her mind.

She closed and locked the gate and went back through the silent courtyard where the moon had reached the pool to turn the drops of water that fell back to the surface into glistening tears. She switched off the lights and mounted the stairs to her room. The plan grew in her mind. Lying awake in the cool glow, she thought it through.

For the next few weeks Nola lived for the mail, although Tom proved to be less than inspired as a letter writer. Yes, he loved her . . . she knew *that*. But it was kind of hard to get it down on paper. If he could talk to her. . . . He was about as busy as a man could get, but every minute, when he didn't have all four hands full of tools, he thought of her. Only forty more days now until he would be in the islands to do some more modification. He would be that much closer to her.

Thirty-nine days, thirty-eight days . . . thirty . . . Nola gave two weeks notice to her supervisor and thanked her stars that Pa would be away on a business trip. Twenty . . . ten . . . she trained the girl who would replace her. She went to class as usual and drove out to the terminal. She wrote to Tom or read in the lounge until time to go home again.

Nine . . . eight . . . She bought a ticket and made reservations through a travel agency. Seven . . . six . . . She cashed a bond and closed out her savings account. Five . . . four . . . three . . . She packed a bag and hid it in the back of her closet.

Mama was looking at her with some bewilderment, and Julie was openly suspicious. "You're up to something," Julie said. "I know it!"

Nola shrugged. "Sure I am. Up to going to class and to work. I'll learn, maybe a little more about business machines. I'll put a tracer on a rush shipment of bathing suits and call a customer to come get a lively tank of lobsters. Then I'll come home and shower and change, and maybe you and I can go to a movie if you don't have a date."

"Oh, hush." Julie lost interest in her premonition.

"Nola, could I wear your blue shorts this afternoon? I'm going to play doubles with Dix and the two cousins that are visiting."

Nola turned away, having no confidence in her ability to look her sister in the eye and lie further. "Sorry, sweetie. I got mustard on them at the drive-in." The blue shorts were packed in that hidden bag.

"It was catsup on mine," Julie said.

Two . . . one! Nola left messages pinned to pillows and got out of the house unseen by either Mama or Faimie, leaving Christy's and Martin's questions unanswered. She waited apprehensively while her bag rode off on the moving belt and disappeared through the flapping doors into the baggage room. Then she lurked in the ladies' lounge until her flight was called. Pa was due home tomorrow, but he might get in early, and she didn't plan to run into him now.

This flight would get her to the West Coast with an hour to spare to make connections. Then she would be flying with all the eagerness of her love to the islands and to Tom.

five 🦋🦋🦋

THE MARRIED LOOK

The chaplain made a note on a pad lying on his desk and looked at Nola. The glint in his eyes puzzled her. "So as soon as your young man arrives— Do I have the name of your hotel? Yes. You were fortunate to get a room there. Nearly nine thousand servicemen on the

Rest and Recreation program come into Honolulu every month, and every one of them wants to overlook the ocean. Go back to your hotel and wait. As soon as he checks in at the fort, he will be told you are here. There's a very brief orientation, and he will be issued an R-and-R identification card that will cut down the cost of your honeymoon by entitling you to discounts."

Nola said hesitantly, "I didn't realize we could be married at once."

"Instant matrimony. The State of Hawaii waives the three-day waiting period for R-and-R men. We recognize that you are young people in a hurry."

Nola felt the flush coming into her face and dropped her eyes before that faintly knowing and understanding gaze. If he arrived at the wrong conclusion from what she had so carefully *not* said—She hadn't wanted to waste a minute.

As he stood up terminating the interview, he looked searchingly at Nola. "Is something wrong? You look a bit disturbed."

"Tom isn't coming on this Rest and Recreation thing," Nola confessed. "I should have made that clear sooner, but there didn't seem a good place to interrupt you."

The chaplain sat down again, frowning. "Your fiancé isn't on R-and-R. He doesn't know you will be here. . . . Well. It would have been much better if you and he had worked out your plans together. Surprises, now—" He paused, then went on carefully, "Some-
62

times girls arrive here under a sad misapprehension."

"Oh, Tom wants to marry me. We planned a wedding when he came home again." Nola's flush really burned her cheeks. "Something came up that made it inadvisable to wait."

The chaplain nodded, aware that many of his young people in a hurry had that sort of thing come up. "We'll hope sincerely that it works out. Good-bye now until" —his eyes went to the note pad—"I see you both at the chapel tomorrow at four."

As she went out into the brilliant sunshine, Nola continued to puzzle over that glint in the chaplain's eyes. Amused? What was funny? She had paid the taxi driver and walked under the palms rustling in the sea breeze to the lanai of her hotel before she identified it. Pa had that same glint in his eyes when he knew she was up to something. The chaplain hadn't believed her careful nonlie about the need for haste.

The waiting was hard. Nola bathed and dressed, then decided against going down to the dining room. Suppose Tom came while she was gone. She took the sandwich and iced tea that room service brought to the balcony. Eating unheedingly she watched the sky darken over Diamond Head and the sea turn from glittering aquamarine to gleaming pewter. As the stars came out, torches flared golden among drifting purple smoke. Late swimmers began to cross the beach in wet, laughing couples, lingering in murmuring embraces in every pool of shadow.

Nola sat with her chin on her hands and her arms folded on the balcony rail and watched them. In a few hours Tom's arms would be around her as tightly as that boy encircled his girl; she would be strained against Tom's chest as closely as that girl was held— The knock at her door brought her to her feet in delighted astonishment. *Tom!* So soon!

She ran across the room and flung the door wide, all her love and longing in her face. It wasn't Tom. A bellboy stared at her around an armful of flowers. Nola was glad of the few seconds bent over her bag getting a tip to compose herself. The boy's sly grin increased her confusion.

She found her father's message among the blossoms after she had closed and locked the door again: *Flowers now; the hairbrush later. Love and exasperation, Mama and Pa.*

Nola laughed, remembering the note she had left on her father's pillow. *Honestly, Pa, I'm not doing this to keep from finishing that darn secretarial course!* Now she and Pa were even.

She spent as much time as possible arranging the flowers, delighting in their fragrance and exotic beauty. She wished she knew their names. After that she prowled restlessly. She was tired and hungry again. And sleepy too. Crossing time zones confused the body's clocks. None of the magazines on the table nor the book she had brought could hold her interest.

Perhaps she could find something at the news counter downstairs.

Turning the rack, she scanned a mystery, a historical novel, a best seller of a few years back that she hadn't read . . . ah, there: *How to Be a Service wife.* She opened that one and then felt the eyes of the two women who were browsing the racks too.

The older one smiled and said, obviously from experience, "You'll find some useful pointers in that."

"I hope so," Nola said earnestly. "I'm going to need all the help I can get!"

"Yes, you will. I suppose you're waiting for the R-and-R plane? I, too. After twenty-five years of Army life, I can tell you that the longer you're married, the more you feel the separation."

The other girl protested. "Oh, Marty, that can't be true!"

"It is, though." The older woman called Marty glanced at her watch and said to Nola, "You'd better trot back upstairs, my dear. That plane should be in by now. You don't want to meet your man with all the world to see."

Tom wouldn't be on the R-and-R plane. He was coming to the air field to make some more changes in that helicopter shield. But Nola didn't want to stand there explaining all that. She thanked the pleasant older woman, said good night and trotted.

Back in her room she read the paperback with determination that failed to convey any meaning to her preoccupation. Finally she gave up and tossed *How to Be a Service Wife* aside. Why was she reading it anyway? She could learn under that best of all teachers, experience. She wouldn't need to know much, for she didn't plan to be a service wife for long. When Tom saw things her way and resigned from the service—

But where was Tom? After another restless hour Nola threw herself on the bed, weeping bitterly. There had been plenty of time for him to receive her message. He wasn't coming. He had decided again that no girl was going to tell him what to do. She had made the same stupid mistake twice. He wasn't coming . . . ever.

She wept until her eyes were red and burning, until her sobs subsided into shuddering, caught breath . . . until her misery sank her into exhausted sleep.

When she struggled up from oblivion, she finally heard the persistent knocking. Blinking at the left-on lights, she found the door and fumbled it open. She woke up then! Tom stood there with expressions of exasperation and delight struggling for mastery on his face. With a loud hiccuping sob Nola flew into his arms.

It was some time later that Tom said, "It would serve you right, you stubborn little cuss, if I didn't marry you. I ought to send you home, jilted and compromised and all that." He grinned at her. "But you're not the type to wear a heavy veil or to become a mysterious recluse, and the times aren't right for that either. You'd more likely dazzle that perishing drama prof and become a famous actress."

"I would not. At least not the actress part. I'm not so good at acting as I thought. I didn't convince the chaplain."

"How's that again?" Tom turned her around so he could see her face.

"It wasn't anything really."

"Come on now. I thought he sounded . . . oh, maybe kind of pitying."

Nola was indignant. "He pitied you because you had to marry me? Why, that old—"

"*Had* to marry you? Nola, what did you tell that man?"

She squirmed away from him. "Nothing actually. I wanted to be sure we could get married right away. If he drew a wrong conclusion, I couldn't help that."

Tom got it. "You let him think I'd have to make you an honest woman? Tom's frown broke up into laughter. "Wait until I tell your mother!"

"You wouldn't dare—" Nola pummeled him, was overpowered and kissed breathless. Tom slid her off his knees then and stood up himself. He was serious again.

"Listen to me, Smarty," he said. "Luck is on your side, or you just might be shipped back home minus a wedding ring, no matter what you told the chaplain. I meant it when I said we were not going to be married while I was shuttling back and forth to the front. But my helicopter shield looks promising enough to be tested in connection with pilot training, so I'll be at Bitter Lake Base while the last class trains there before the base is closed down. We can live there—"

Nola stopped holding her breath. "*We*? We! I can go with you? Even if we have to live in sin?" She backed away from him in mock terror. "Tom, you *said—*"

Nola stared in such horror that Tom stopped his advance and looked over his own shoulder. "What's wrong?"

She had caught sight of herself in the mirror. "Why didn't you tell me?" Nola covered her face with her hands. "I look frightful! I slept in my dress—just look at me! No, don't! And I cried until my eyes are red, and my face is puffy and tear streaked. Oh, Tom, just when I so wanted to look nice for you!"

She was back in his arms again. "You don't look nice," Tom said. "I doubt that you are nice. But you look beautiful."

When Nola looked into a mirror again at three the next afternoon, she really looked beautiful for Tom. Her white dress was simple and very young. So was the head bow with a small ruffle of veil. When she lifted a hand to straighten a fold, the lei of flowers Tom had chosen wreathed her with a heady fragrance. The sweetness brought to Nola's mind an opposite—the light tart scent of the lemon thyme in the courtyard at home. But that home was in the past now; in the present was the grown-up home of marriage.

She left the Bride's Room and met Tom, waiting in the chapel. Thrilling with the music in her breast and seeing his love in his eyes she hurried into her new home in his heart.

She wakened first next morning, instantly aware of Tom sleeping beside her. She propped her head on her hand, memorizing every detail of his beloved face.

Tom lay with one brown hand tucked under his cheek, a cheek that was hollowed. He was much thinner. He had said very little more than that it was bad out there. Nola said a prayer of gratitude for his safe return and thankfulness that he need not go back again.

Tom's eyebrows were feathers. She resisted the impulse to trace them with a forefinger. She shouldn't wake him. He must be starved for sleep after the apprehensive semislumber of the outposts. Sleeping like a child. . . . No. She corrected her thought. There was nothing childish about Tom, very little really that was boyish. Tom was a man. Nola suddenly felt very young. Humbly she promised herself and him that she would be a woman now that she was a wife. She would put away childish things—

Tom's eyes had opened. She kept staring at him, her thoughts continuing into words. "Oh, darling, I mean to be a good wife—"

"Then come here, woman!" Tom said.

Nola pressed her forehead to the window for a last glimpse of Diamond Head falling behind the plane. As they climbed until the sparkling ocean withdrew under a coverlet of cottony cloud, she turned back to Tom, her hand tight in his.

"Six days wasn't half enough."

"The world was made in that much time," Tom said.

"So was ours." Nola knew she voiced his thought too.

They were silent for a time, their hands linked as their thoughts had been. Then Tom said, "We'll come back again. Probably many times. Join the service and see the world."

Nola said hopefully, "When the war is over—"

"—the Air Force will still be keeping the peace in foreign lands," Tom finished.

Without us, Nola said to herself. This wasn't the time to talk about her plans for their future.

"You know," she said confidently, "in another week we could have made heaven too!"

In a few hours, they were greeting Nola's family, planning to visit for a few days and pick up Nola's things before going to Bitter Lake Base.

"Oh, Mama! Oh, Papa! Oh, Julie!" Nola said between and around the welcoming arrival kisses. "I'm so happy!"

"Then why are you crying, Sister?" Christy and Martin asked.

Nola scooped them into her arms and kissed them lavishly. "Because I'm so happy."

Set down again, Christy and Martin looked at each other. "We guess you have to be grown-up to be happy in such a silly way."

Pa and Tom shook hands seriously, then grinned at each other as Nola went back into her mother's and sister's embraces. "She's a handful," Pa said. "Strong willed and stubborn."

"The word I had in mind is 'bull-headed.' " As Tom went to Louise, he added, "We'll have to concede the first round is hers."

"Eloping solo is a pretty sneaky way to drop out," Julie said to Nola as she kissed her.

"Let's go home." Louise Foret started the small ones. "I need some coffee after all this cryptic conversation, and Faimie said dinner couldn't wait too long. We'll wait in the car, Gerald, while you and Tom claim the luggage."

With Christy and Martin on either hand, Nola looked over their heads to Tom. Shared understanding flowed between them almost visibly. Turning away with the children, Nola felt a responding warmth flooding through her body.

That shared thought had told her that she and Tom would never be separated again. Not really. Not by time or space. One went one way, the other went another way, but by the mystery of love they would be together.

That was the way Mama and Pa could look at each other with a single thought between them. It was a married look.

six

INVOLUNTARY VOLUNTEER

Nola sat on a packing box, elbows propped on knees and her chin on her fists. The box was the last. She should get it out of the middle of the floor before Tom came home. There was probably nothing she would ever need in it anyway, she thought wearily. What trappings of a civilized life would be useful in such a place?

Through the uncurtained window she could see across the slowly rising desert plain to the distant mountains. Their quarters were in the last row of housing at the sandy, windy Bitter Lake Base where Tom worked on his helicopter shielding in connection with replacement-pilot training.

Racing across Nola's view, a black girl with her head tied in a kerchief, her slimness clothed in shirt and shorts, chased a little boy capering and squealing with delight in his escape. They came back in a minute at a slower pace with the laughing child riding his mother's shoulders. The girl looked in with frank curiosity.

"Hi!" she said. "I'm Fran Bishop, next door. Are you straightened up yet?"

"Hi. Twice. One for each of you." Nola reached through the unscreened window where the air conditioner would go to tickle the little boy's bare foot. "No, I'm not very straight. Just goofing off. Sitting here admiring the"—she paused to let the inflection put quotes around the words—"lovely view."

"A terrible hole, isn't it?" the girl called Fran said cheerfully. "Dick says it's east of nothing, west of nowhere and in the middle of trouble! That's service life for you. Well, see you later. I've got to take this youngun back to his spinach."

Nola thought the "terrible hole" was all that Fran had said. She stared at the endless expanse that looked

73

flat but wasn't, at the thorny brush curiously spaced equidistant from its neighbors. Sandy rock ledges shouldered through sandy soil sparkling with minute flakes of mica. At the horizon, where hot white sky met hot, gray-white earth, the air shimmered with heat.

Nola thought longingly of home. It was an hour later there. The family would be drifting into the sleepy coolness of the courtyard after eating Faimie's excellent lunch. They might have had a shrimp and crab salad with hot rolls and fig ice cream. Nola swallowed hungrily. She should eat something too.

Opening the refrigerator, she stared in at the eggs and bacon, the chopped meat and the cheese, then shut the door again. She wasn't hungry enough to eat any of that. Or to like eating alone either. Tom wouldn't be back until evening.

"You thought you'd see a lot of Tom if you were married to him," Nola told herself. "But Tom's married to his work. Did you ever get fooled!"

She got up then and attacked the box with hammer and screw driver. When she had opened a corner, she saw that it contained clothing. The first thing that came out was the white dress she had been married in and that she had worn again when Mama and Pa gave a reception at home for them. Nola folded her arms around the soft silk and waltzed herself around the room singing dolefully, "Oh, how we danced on the night we were wed. . . ."

If they could have stayed at home, the parties would have gone on for a month at least. All the Foret relatives, her godfather, Mama's people, the cousins in the country and the family friends would have entertained for her and Tom. It was bad enough to miss all that fun, but Tom had thanked God they had "escaped."

"You mean you're glad?" she had said indignantly.

"Well, I'm sorry if all that whirl meant something to you, sugar." Tom had reached out to perch her on his knees. "What's wrong with two people who love each other being alone together? What else is a honeymoon? I like it this way."

"Oh, I want to be with you, Tom. That's the honeymoon."

Nola meant it too, with all her heart. But as they kissed, she couldn't help wishing that she could be with Tom someplace else . . . someplace like back home.

Next morning she saw Tom off after an early breakfast and plunged into nest making. The quarters had a stove and a refrigerator, a sofa and an armchair, a bed, a table, two stools and red painted walls. Something had to be done.

During the next week, Nola found she had make-do abilities she hadn't imagined. She borrowed tools from the craft shop and cut a wooden, almost circular piece from one of the packing boxes. The circle nailed on top of another box and skirted in blue corduroy lifted the

75

spirits of the living room. She rented a portable sewing machine in town and made slipcovers for the deplorable sofa and chair and pads for the stools.

"It was like making dresses for an elephant," Nola wrote in her letter to Mama that week. "I wouldn't want you to look too closely. Wherever I couldn't sew, I pinned or stapled, but the effect is good anyway. I bought mattress ticking for the slip covers and used the same stuff at the windows. Scraps of the blue corduroy helped the stools quite a bit."

When Tom came home one evening, she was cross-legged on the living room floor, painting tassels around a red-painted rug patterned with blue and white squiggles. "Mind the paint, darling," she called. "How does it look?"

"I thought I'd walked into the wrong house," Tom said. "Can I hire you out so we'll have a second income?"

Nola laughed. "It's a thought. I'll have to do something or expire from boredom with you gone all day. I'll start on the bedroom next, so we won't feel like we're living inside a red balloon."

Tom lifted her by her elbows, paintbrush and all. As he kissed her, he said, "I don't find a thing wrong with the way we're living."

Nola didn't either just then. After a moment she pushed Tom away. "If you don't want the stew to burn—" She wailed, "Look what I did to your shirt!

Take it off, and I'll ask the girl next door how to get the paint out. She's the kind who can cope."

After dinner—the stew hadn't scorched and the biscuits had risen—Nola went next door to ask about the stained shirt.

"Lighter fluid will probably take it out," Fran thought. "Shall we walk over to the thrift shop together tomorrow?"

"Thanks just the same," Nola said, "but I have some other things to do in the morning."

Fran widened her eyes. "Oh, what you *said!*"

"I mean I'm busy trying to make that dump we're dumped in a little less dumpier—"

Fran shook her head vigorously. "It won't go down with the Colonel's Lady."

"Mrs. Slayton? Why should she care?"

Fran sighed. "I keep forgetting this is your first post. Listen, honey. When the Colonel's Lady says, 'Hop!' all the officers' wives make like frogs. The wives of lieutenants (that's me) hop the fastest and the farthest, but captain's wives come next. Your name is on the list to staff the thrift shop tomorrow and Thursday. I saw it right below mine. The Colonel's Lady makes up the list believing that responsibility is *so* good for the younger wives. And we Judy O'Gradys better believe it too."

"You mean I *have* to go in the morning? To do what?"

"Let's say it would be wiser if you went in the morning just like the list says. Volunteers—ha!—from the Officers' Wives Club (you belong to that automatically) and the Noncommissioned Officers Ladies Auxiliary staff the shop. People bring in things to sell on consignment, and a percentage from the sale is kept by the shop. The percentage keeps the post nursery and various community projects going."

"So I'll make a contribution to the nursery fund."

"It isn't that simple," Fran said patiently. "The Colonel's Lady *says*. So you'd better go, for your husband's sake if not yours."

"Well, all right, I'll go. But I don't see the sense of it."

Fran looked at Nola sharply. "Are you just doing time, or are you in for life?"

Nola blinked, then understood. "That depends," she said carefully. "On whether you're asking me or Tom."

"Like that, huh? I don't say you don't have lots of company. But long term or short term, who are you to tell the Colonel's Lady how to run the service?"

Nola repeated part of the conversation to Tom. "Fran was exaggerating, wasn't she? Especially that bit about what I do or don't do affecting your career?"

"Put it this way, honey. If I were a military genius, any little flaps you have with the Colonel's Lady wouldn't keep me from promotion. Since I'm just a run-of-the-mill soldier, sure to put plenty of mistakes on my record myself, any you add won't help."

78

Nola made an impatient sound, then repented of it. "Okay, Boss, I'll go. And you watch. I'll have the lady brass eating out of my hand. If soft soap is needed to guarantee your advancement, you'll be the youngest general in history. *Sir!*"

Tom spanked her smartly on the area thrust backward by the exaggeration of her salute. "I don't doubt the part about the Colonel's Lady eating out of your hand, but there may be a bit more to the rest of it. You'll like Maggie Slayton when you come to know her. She and I have been on post together twice now. She sort of mothers the bachelor officers."

"I'll take care of your mothering from now on," Nola said firmly.

Next day, she went with Fran to the thrift shop, where they had only an occasional customer during the morning. Nola chatted with Fran and regretted that she hadn't provided something to pass the time.

"I wish I'd brought my knitting, if I had some knitting to bring," Nola said. She roamed around the room looking at the stock on the shelves. "Goodness, there's enough crystal here to outfit twenty brides!"

Fran glanced up from her clicking needles. "Probably did."

"These are wedding presents?"

"Mostly. Everybody's short of money—let me tell you, it's rough in the ranks. I should know, because Dick came up from there to be commissioned. And we know the base will be deactivitated soon. Are the girls going to box up the wedding presents and ship them home to Mother? She's probably short of storage space herself."

Nola rang a goblet carefully with a fingernail. "Seems a shame. Such pretty things. Who buys them?"

"People drive out from town looking for bargains. Or some of the wives whose men are going where you can take dependents—like Germany—may buy something if it's cheap enough. Hey, we've got a customer."

The two girls came in and looked hesitantly around the room. The taller one, visibly sparking with indignation, hovered protectingly over the small girl whose dark eyes swam with tears and whose pregnancy had stretched her suit unbecomingly. Nola and Fran exchanged a questioning glance.

Fran called casually to them. "Just look around, will you? Everything is priced, but if we can help—"

The taller girl spotted the rack of maternity clothes and took her friend over. They sorted out a dress, a coat, some slacks and tops, began holding them and measuring around.

Fran and Nola came over. "Would you like to try things on?" Fran asked. "There's a dressing room over there."

In a few minutes the tall girl came out with the dress, shaking her head. "Doesn't do," she said, rehanging it and searching the rack for another.

"What's wrong?" Fran asked in a whisper. "How about this one? It will be good for summer."

The tall girl shook her clenched fists. Her low voice was fierce. "If I ever see him again—God forbid! I'll kill him! I will!"

There was no doubt she meant what she said. The other two stared at her in consternation.

"She's the *sweetest* little dunce! This soldier married her—" The furious girl interrupted herself: "I'll bet you any money he's married two or three times. He's probably played this trick before! Got her pregnant right away, of course. Then his time was up, he gets separated from the service and walks out on that poor kid. Kisses her good-bye, says something like, 'It's been nice knowing you, honey, but you just wouldn't fit in back home.' Then the heel drives off in the car *she's* been working to keep up the payments on and leaves her without even a rag to go back to her mother in!"

She took the dress from Fran, assessed it fiercely and went back into the dressing room. Nola and Fran stared at each other.

"Can't somebody do something?" Nola asked.

Fran sighed. "Like what? He's out, and who knows where he's gone?"

"Are there any others?"

"Like the heel, you mean? More than you like to think about. There are a few rats in every haystack, you know. No more in military haystacks than in civilian ones. It's probably a good riddance. The life is hard enough when you've got a good man like you and I have."

The two girls came from the dressing room, the little dark one neat in the summer-weight dress, her friend with the other garments over her arm.

"Doesn't she look nice?" the tall one asked. "Lupe, you want these, don't you? They come to under twenty dollars. You've got to have something to wear."

"How lucky!" Nola said brightly. "We have twenty dollars in a special fund for emergencies. Here"—she took the garments—"let me wrap these for you."

She let Fran receive the tearful thanks, going with Lupe to the door. Lupe's friend dropped back to mutter, "God bless. That was probably your grocery money, huh? I've dipped about as far as I can into mine."

Fran came back and sat down to her knitting again. Over the clicking needles she said finally, "I told her to go to see the Colonel's Lady. There really is a fund for emergency transportation. I'm glad there was a good assortment of maternity clothes in Lupe's size. We don't do such a booming business in hatching stuff since The Pill. That playpen came in last month, and it's still here."

As if mentioning it had brought her, a girl came in to ask if they had a playpen. "I shouldn't buy a thing with Jack going to Vietnam so soon," she told Fran. "But the baby is crawling everyplace and the floor is so splintery. Tideover service doesn't have one they can lend just now."

Nola had heard that voice before. She watched the

girl rounding the playpen, shaking it to test its strength, and recognized her. "Dottie Broussard! At high school. In English class and senior play."

"It's . . . Nola?" Dottie's voice was doubtful. "Nola what?"

"Nola Foret. Now Cartright."

"Of course." Dottie caught Nola's hands. "I'm Dottie Harper now. Oh, I'm so glad to see someone from home. You just came?"

Nola who had scorned blushing brides as clichés felt herself reddening. "We were married six weeks ago in Hawaii as Tom came back from Vietnam."

"You lucky thing! To have him back, I mean. This awful war that nobody can believe in! I don't know what I'm going to do when Jack goes. Neither of us has any family to speak of. I have a great aunt, and Jack has some cousins, but I don't know them. With the baby it will be hard for me to work, for a full-time sitter would about use up any salary I could earn. I wish I'd learned something in school that pays real good. I wanted to be a nurse but it didn't work out."

Nola included Fran in the conversation. "We were talking about the post nursery when you came in, Dottie. Can't you put the baby there?"

"Oh, I will. Butch has been there a few times already and loved it. But it won't be for long, you know. Wives have to move off post after their men leave. We may get moved out even earlier when the base is de-activated."

"We've got a problem." Nola frowned over it. "Fran, can't we think of some way to sell this stuff faster? And keep the nursery open longer?"

Swooping around the shop, Nola chose a blonde wig and clapped it over her own dark head. Then she took a satin stole from a rack and wrapped it around her shoulders. Striking an attitude she swished and postured down the room.

"Why don't we have a style show?"

She wheeled sharply to prance down her imaginary runway. And found herself nose to nose with an elegant woman dressed exactly right for a morning in the thrift shop. But that formidable person was smiling.

"What an excellent idea, Mrs. Cartright! I do like my wives to show some initiative. Now, since it was your idea, you're the logical choice to be chairman for the show!"

seven ❦❦❦

SUCCESS DOESN'T PAY

Nola stared indignantly at Tom. "It isn't funny. Now I must plan a style show, write a script and get girls to model a lot of secondhand clothes. Tom Cartright, stop laughing!"

"It's so neat. The way the Colonel's Lady made the punishment fit the crime."

"She couldn't have heard anything I said."

"Want to bet? Precious little gets said or done on this base that Maggie Slayton doesn't know about. Usually ten minutes before it happens."

"Happens . . . happening! That's it! That's the way I'll do the style show. 'Happenings at the Thrift Shop,' or maybe 'Happenings and Hand-me-downs.' And I'll ask the Colonel's Lady to model."

Collecting pen and paper, Nola stopped to laugh. "Pa was so insistent that I finish that secretarial course before I could even mention drama. And here I am directing my own production!"

Tom was serious now. "There's no discharge in this war, you know."

"So?"

"You can't drop this style-show thing if you get tired of it, or if it gets hard or bores you."

"You've been listening to Pa. I'll show you both I can finish something. You watch, Tom Cartright. I'll make you proud of me."

In the next week, with much groaning and chewing of pencil tips, Nola wrote a script for the style show. She settled on five scenes: *Happening at Home* (mops, scrub buckets, curtains to hang and shirts and shorts). *Happening in the Hills* (a picnic, slacks and sweaters, sunglasses, sandals, shovels and spades to dig up a treasure—Nola stopped there to write in a new idea:

the discovered treasure chest would open to show the half-bushel of costume jewelry that wasn't selling at the thrift shop. Good!). *Happening with Hospitality* (a first dinner party given by a nervous bride—"note to me," Nola added, "don't assign any butterfingers to this scene, not with all that lovely crystal"). For the fourth scene, *Happening with Half-Pints* (cute kids, playpens—Dottie may have to bring that one back for the day—potty chairs and cribs). And *Happening on a Honeymoon* (a lot of the impractical frilly stuff girls got at lingerie showers—"note to me, put on enough pancake makeup to hide your blushes." Wigs could go there too).

Now if she could keep it light and amusing . . .

She worked on the commentary with the sewing machine running up more rent than seams and the wallpaper for the bedroom stacked reproachfully un-pasted in a corner. Meals ran largely to poached eggs in cheese sauce, creamed chicken on toast and even TV dinners. But the show was taking shape and was going to be *good*.

One evening Tom found her intently running tucks in an outdated evening dress to make a minilength. After he had kissed her, he asked, "What's for dinner?" with a doubtful eye on the cold stove and uncluttered kitchen.

Nola measured another tuck. "I'll whip up something in a minute. I want to finish this—"

Tom took the dress out of her hands. "I don't feel for

'something.' Let's go over to the club. I know you're working very hard on that blasted show, but I've had it with quick little messes."

She was outraged. "Messes! Well, don't blame me. It's the Colonel's Lady's fault that I have no time to prepare a nightly banquet for Your High Mightiness!"

"Come off it, honey. I know how busy you are. But that doesn't mean I couldn't eat a steak. How about you?"

Nola was suddenly ravenous. She could stand on her pride and refuse to go, but Tom would go off without her, drat him. The prospect of eating tuna casserole alone wasn't inviting.

She pummeled Tom vigorously. "I'll remember what you said about my cooking. Look for me to spice it up with a nice dose of arsenic one of these days!"

Tom caught her hands as she resisted and pulled her down on the couch beside him. The mock battle set them both panting before it ended in a long kiss.

They still lingered over their steaks when the colonel and his lady came into the club dining room. They saw the young Cartrights and nodded to them pleasantly. Almost immediately Maggie Slayton got up again.

Her voice carried across the tables. "No, don't come with me. Go ahead and order. If you come, they'll have to let their food get cold."

Tom told Nola under his breath, "That's thoughtful of her, you've got to admit."

Bearing down upon them, as Tom got to his feet, the Colonel's Lady said, "I'll only take a minute. I just want to tell you, Tom, you have a nice girl here."

"I think so," Tom agreed.

"With a little time and training she will make a good service wife."

Nola longed to laugh but dared not. Then suddenly she found herself proud of the backhanded praise.

The Colonel's Lady went on, "A general's wife told me once of six qualities a good service wife should have. Nola gets full marks already for three of them. She has enthusiasm, ability to work and *purpose*." Her voice underlined that. "Two of the best purposes are creativity and service, and she's demonstrated those by the work she's doing on the style show. I just wanted you to know, Tom, that I'm very pleased with her so far."

She nodded and smiled and went back to her husband. Nola and Tom stared past each other. Tom muffled something that wasn't a cough but didn't dare to be anything else in his napkin; Nola finished a bite of steak with stern concentration.

"Don't look at me," she begged. "Or I'll start giggling and disgrace us both. I wonder what the other three qualities are?"

"We could take our coffee in the lounge," Tom said. "I'd guess you still need Buttering Up (Simple and Advanced), Noncooking I and II and Husband Neglect, Plain and Fancy."

"You hush! We'll have a pot of coffee at home. I really should get back to that script I'm so creative and pleasing about."

Tom signed the check. Then, passing the colonel's table, they said respectfully, "Good evening, sir. Good evening, ma'am" and escaped. Safely in their car, they fell into each other's arms and laughed all the way home.

But that was the last time the style show brought laughter to Nola. Mostly it brought work of the hardest kind. She thought often it would be twice as easy to do it all herself. Then there would be no asking someone to do something, riding herd on her to make sure the work was done and pitching in at the last minute to finish it. She desperately needed that course in Buttering Up, Simple and Advanced. You just couldn't praise effort enough. Committees! Especially women on committees!

The style show was, however, an unqualified success. More than 150 women lunched, laughed at the amusing commentary Nola made and actually bought many of the props and clothing when the show was over. The post nursery benefited, and the Colonel's Lady was gratified.

"So I'm sunk," Nola told Tom. "Success doesn't pay.

Because I'm so good at it I can just keep on being good at it. Goody, goody."

"It won't go on forever," Tom said. "After this group of pilots finishes, we'll be assigned somewhere else. This base is due to be deactivated."

Nola was too engrossed in her grievances to really listen. "I'm sure to be rewarded by being made vice-president in charge of wives. Why don't I keep my mouth shut? Tom, what would happen if I just didn't show up at the thrift shop when it's my turn?"

"I hardly think you'd get life imprisonment. You might get confined to barracks."

"She wouldn't dare! Still—" She looked at the not-quite-decorated living room and the bedroom not even begun. "I'm almost ready to chance it. Then I could finish up here."

"I wouldn't if I were you."

"What will I do, Tom, after the house is halfway livable? You'll be gone all day."

"Sure. I have to work. So could you."

"Doing what?"

"That's for you to decide. Whatever you do best; whatever interests you most."

Nola shook her head. "No matter how I gussy up this place, I don't want to go on doing such. And the thrift shop really doesn't interest me. I guess I got married before I decided what I liked best. Besides you! Maybe service life isn't it."

"Give it a chance, honey."

"I can hang around dreary quarters," Nola said pensively. "Or go out and crunch around in the sand. I can serve polite little teas to the other wives when they come to lift their eyebrows at our makeshift domestic arrangements. And I'll have a dandy chance of having the Colonel's Lady come before I get the bed made to haul me off to work in the thrift shop."

"Hey, you're real bitter tonight. I know Maggie Slayton can be a pain, but she can be kind too. You have to remember she is the Old Man's wife. That makes her a built-in boss for the wives. R.H.I.P."

"How's that again?" Nola said.

Tom laughed. "*Rank Has Its Privileges*. It's a service catchword. You'll find it all evens out. If we pull lousy duty, the next go round we may get a plum. Same way with a post. You get good ones and bad ones. Every place has its drawbacks and its good points. Actually, any post is about what you make it. So get to work doing something useful and important—important to you, that is. It doesn't matter how it looks to anyone else. End of lecture."

"Ha!" said Nola scornfully. "I should get in a glow over needlepoint or Siamese cats or learning Russian!" She hesitated. "Tom, do we have to stay in?"

His eyebrows raised in question. "How do you mean?"

"You could resign. There must be plenty of openings for engineers outside the service. Then we could live in nice places and be together more and—"

92

"Now cut it out," Tom said gruffly. "Nobody made me join. I happen to believe this is a great country doing its best most times to make the world a better place to live in. There has never been a nation in history that has poured out more blood and gold less selfishly. About all I can do is my bit to keep the nation safe while the work goes on. But that's an important bit, and I'm proud to be doing it until we can fight the war through to peace—"

"I even love you when you're mad at me," Nola said meekly.

Tom grabbed her then and, half in fun and half in exasperation, turned her across his knees. Before he could swat her, she wiggled upright in his arms and pulled his head down until their lips met. The exasperation and the bitterness disappeared in the love-making.

But next morning Nola was sleepy and disgruntled over her breakfast coffee. Around a yawn, she asked, "Why does a field problem have to start at dawn?"

Tom turned a page in the manual at his elbow before he looked up. By that time Nola had read the title of the booklet and asked another question. "*How to March on an Azimuth*. What's an azimuth?"

"The arc of the horizon that a vertical plane passing through a heavenly body makes with the meridian of the place of observation," Tom recited glibly.

"Heavenly body as in pinup?"

Tom looked pained. "It's a method of getting there

from here. Suppose you have a downed helicopter crew. You must have some way of knowing which way to get out."

Nola saw mentally a raveled skein of men, some of them wounded, all of them exhausted, threading a cautious way through jungle. Was that Tom leading the way—she hastily turned off the picture. She wouldn't think about him having to go back there—

Tom ruffled her hair as he got up. Her closed eyes looked like sleepiness to him. "Back to the sack, honey. You can have a real long nap. I'll be flying all day practicing casualty pickups."

Nola caught his arm around her shoulders when he would have taken it away. "Tom, I wanted to ask you something. Tom, I'm really tired. Could I go home for a few days?"

"Home? You are home."

"Oh, you know what I mean. Home as of childhood. Just for a few days? To see Mama and Pa and Julie and the little 'uns and not have to think what's for dinner." She thought of another reason. "I could get some of my things that I need here."

Tom shook his head. "Don't bring anything more. You'd just have to pack them again. How come you don't want to stay with me? You were plenty anxious a few weeks ago."

"I still am. My goodness, I'm not asking for a trial separation. I just want to go for a few days. What's so big about that?"

94

"To be honest, I don't want you to go." Then he caught sight of his watch and kissed her again hurriedly. "We'll talk about it tonight, honey. 'Bye now."

Nola sat on at the breakfast table when he had clattered out of the house. She finished her coffee and started to pour another cup, then thought better of it. She began stacking the dishes in the sink, then stopped halfway. Dismissing the eggy plates and the coffee cups with an airy gesture, she said aloud, "You wait right there until noon. Now it's back to bed for Nola."

With her head buried in the pillow Nola heard the knocking. She opened her eyes halfway, willing the knocker away. *Knock, knock, knock. , , ,* Pause. *Knock, knock, knock. . . .* She groaned and sat on the edge of the bed. It couldn't be noon already. And the dishes holding her to her promise wouldn't make that much noise coming to get her.

She found her robe and padded off on bare feet. Muttering to herself, she went to the kitchen door. Opening it, she said peevishly, "Tran, if you woke me up to borrow a cup of something—" There was no one on that doorstep.

The knocking was at the front door. Nola reversed herself, still mutttering. "Who on earth—"

The opened door revealed the Colonel's Lady, her hand raised to knock again. She looked concerned and took Nola's arm as she came in, not waiting to be invited.

"I *knew* you were ill. Dear me, child, you look bad."

Her glance over Nola's shoulder took in the cluttered kitchen and the open door that revealed the unmade bed. "You must have been sick since early morning. Why didn't Tom call me?"

Nola shook her bewildered head. "Why should he have bothered you?"

"I'm sure it upset him too." The Colonel's Lady smiled. "Honestly there's nothing more useless than a man around sickness. But I could have reassured you. It isn't serious at all, just awfully unpleasant. Fortunately it doesn't last long. Doctors can do so much much more for you than they could in my day."

"I'm not sick," Nola protested. "What makes you think I am? I just wanted to sleep in for a change." She could see the kitchen clock. Nine thirty. "Not that I did so very."

Her visitor sat up straight as a ramrod on the slip-covered couch. Nola wondered if the spring she had retied with an amateur's optimism hadn't nudged Maggie.

"You didn't come to the thrift shop this morning because you wanted to sleep late?" The warmth had gone out of that assured voice.

"Oh, my goodness," said Nola. "Was it my turn today? I guess I just didn't feel for selling secondhand clothes two days in a row. There was hardly likely to be a crush at the shop, was there? After the style show? And I have an engagement a little later." She tried to make the lie convincing.

"Something you'd rather do, I'm sure," the Colonel's Lady said with ice in her voice. Then she told Nola a few home truths and went away closing the door firmly behind her.

Like a sleepwalker Nola went to the telephone. She might catch Tom at the hangars coming back to get another load of something. She did. She talked fiercely for a few minutes, then paused, listened to a few words from the other end of the wire and then slammed the receiver down with a crash.

She went into the kitchen, gathering the dishes from the table and stacking them in the sink. She was standing with her arms in soapy water, with tears of rage rolling down her cheeks when Fran came followed by Dottie Harper.

"Has Her Nibs gone?" Fran whispered. "We couldn't see her car out front. Let's hope she doesn't go back to the shop. We closed down an hour earlier. She'll *kill* us. What on earth happened, Nola?"

Nola sniffed and wiped her nose on her sleeve. "She l-looked down her nose at me! All sweet and sour at the same time like lemonade and she s-said"—Nola mimicked a tart decisive voice "'You know, my dear, when Tom brought you to the base, I had high hopes for you. Tom is such a darling. He d-deserves a good wife. I was glad to believe I was mistaken in thinking you were too young and immature when you did such a fine job with the style show. But after this irresponsibility of not showing up to do your work because you

97

wanted to sleep late—well, I conclude that you're too childish for marriage and always will be.' How dare she say such things to me!"

Fran and Dottie looked at each other in consternation. Older in experience, they knew it might not actually go down on Tom's fitness record that his wife had been impertinent to his commander's wife, but it would get around the small tight world of the base by word of mouth. And the rumor if not the fact might even follow him to his next assignment.

"Has Tom been home? Have you talked to him?" Dottie asked.

"He hasn't been home, but I had him on the phone and"—she stopped and caught her breath in a sob— "he was just as bad as she was! I told him how the Colonel's Lady thought I was sick and was all honey and pie telling me it wouldn't last long—" Nola broke off as realization and rage struggled on her face. "Why, that nosey old busybody! She the same as ordered me to have a baby! I suppose she'll get Tom drummed out of the service when she finds out I'm not. Anyway, Tom didn't laugh or tell me to forget it. He just stood there at the phone and breathed at me. When I repeated what she'd said about me being childish and too young for marriage, he said, 'She may be right.' And he hung up!"

Nola stood at the sink another moment, then splashed a cup into the cooling water and ran into the bedroom. "You can come help me pack, if you want," she called over her shoulder. "I'm going into town and take the first plane that has an empty seat."

"Where are you going?" Dottie was anxious.

"I told Tom this morning I wanted to go home for a little while, but now I've changed my mind. I'm going for a *long* while. Maybe from now on!" Nola wrestled a bag down from the closet shelf and began throwing clothes into it.

"Now, now . . . calm down," Fran said. "Don't rush off in a twitch. Wait and talk to Tom tonight. You can work it out together. Everybody has a first quarrel, honey. And it's wonderful to make up."

"I'm sure Tom will approve of your going to see your family," Dottie said.

"I don't care now if he approves or not. As I see it, we're just about finished." Nola sniffed loudly. "So I quit."

"*Divorce?*" Dottie asked in a shocked voice.

"Of course she doesn't mean divorce," Fran said sharply. "Neither do I, but, oh, boy, have I ever dreamed of murder! Plenty times I could kill that lug I'm married to, but I wouldn't give him the satisfaction of divorcing him!"

"No, I couldn't divorce Tom," Nola said. "But I'm sick of living in this place"—she visibly scorned the little house where she had so happily tried out her nest-making instincts—"of being buried alive in a hole like this—" She began to cry again. "I won't live with Tom unless he gets into work that can be done in a civilized place and where the boss's wife doesn't crack a whip day and night over the poor cowering slaves!"

"What about Tom's career? His commission?"

Nola tossed her head. "He can resign, can't he? He will have to decide between the service and me."

"He may make a choice you won't be able to live with, either," Fran muttered.

"Jack thinks Tom is a fine officer," Dottie said. "Born to it, were his words."

"Well, I wasn't born to be an officer's wife," Nola snapped at her friend.

Dottie was honestly bewildered. "Why did you marry him?"

Nola pushed her hair off her forehead fretfully. "How do I know! Maybe I didn't really see the officer, except to find the uniform so becoming. I was really, truly in love for the first time. It was all so thrilling and absorbing and confusing, I didn't know what I was doing."

"If you'd stopped to think," Fran said. "You weren't being fair to Tom."

Nola's eyes were bright with anger. "So what's fair about love? Especially what's fair about marriage?" The angry sparks drowned in the tears that welled up in her eyes. "I don't want to talk about it anymore."

eight 🖤🖤🖤

COOL IT

When Nola came home so unexpectedly, Mama was surprised, Pa was astonished and Julie was suspicious.

"I do think you might have let us know," Mama fretted. "I don't have a free minute all this week. Why didn't you write or phone so I could have refused some of these engagements?"

"I didn't decide—well, things came up," Nola said vaguely. "I didn't know I could come until the last minute."

"What things?" Pa wanted to know. "For a girl who couldn't stand to be separated from her lover long enough to have a decent wedding, you've left him rather soon."

"We did *too* have a decent wedding!" Nola was stung into a retort. "I thought you'd be glad to see me. But if you don't want me here, I can turn around and go back."

"Oh, I am. I am glad to see you. And your mother is delighted," Pa said. But he drank his coffee thoughtfully. Nola knew he wasn't completely satisfied with her explanation.

Julie was franker. "Why don't you just admit you had a fight with Tom? And came home to cool it?"

"So what if I did? It wasn't so much Tom as the Colonel's Lady—" Nola stopped but she had already said too much not to say more.

The whole story had to come out. And even to Nola's ears it sounded feeble. "I couldn't let her push me around like that, could I? I'd worked like a horse on that blasted style show for her, and then she talked to me like that! When Tom agreed with her, that was too much. What else could I do?"

"You could have stayed where you belong." Pa was grimmer than Nola had ever seen him. "I mean your home, not ours. Louise, we will be doing less than our duty toward this bull-headed daughter if we don't put her on a planc headed back. Right now!"

"Now, Gerald." Mama was troubled but, Nola felt, more than half in agreement with Pa. "Surely Nola can stay here in her own home for a few days until she gets her emotions under control."

"A married woman's home is where her husband is," Pa said shortly. "I'd like to remind your daughter, madam, that marriage isn't something you drop out of like a course of study you no longer wish to pursue."

"Now, Gerald," Louise said again. "I'm sure Nola doesn't look at marriage like that. . . ." But her voice wasn't as sure as her words. "Suppose we all go to bed now and get a good night's sleep. In the morning everything will look different and probably better."

To Nola's opening eyes everything did look different. Her room seemed strange instead of feeling familiar. A faint breeze still damp with wisps of dawn fog stirred the curtains at the floor-length windows. Outside, the dark, leathery oaks that shaded the garden to a perpetual half-light scarcely moved a leaf. Insect hum and bird song traced a delicate pattern of sound over the background rumble of traffic outside the wall. How different this awakening from that at home.

This breeze was languid; the other was brisk. Here everything would progress as usual if she stayed in bed all day; there everything would come to a screeching halt. Nola decided she didn't want to go on with the contrasts and turned her face into her pillow.

The tap at the door was Christy, opening the door for Martin stepping carefully with a tray. "We brought your breakfast, Sister," they said. Arranging the tray over Nola's lap, they splashed the coffee as they hugged her.

"Why didn't you wake us up when you came last night?" they asked. "We wanted to see you right away."

Nola hugged them to her on either side. "You were asleep. And I was hot and tired."

Martin understood. "So Mama told you to take a bath and get ready for bed. That's what she tells us."

"Especially when we're tired and cranky," Christy added.

Martin was looking his older sister over critically. "You don't look very glad, Sister. Didn't you want to come home? Are you sad because Tom didn't come with you? I like Tom."

"Oh, so do I. Tom had to work. So he had to stay at home . . . our home, his and mine. But I am glad to be here at this home."

Nola hid their puzzled faces against her shoulders with another hug. How could she explain to them that "home" was movable? That what had been home a few weeks ago wasn't home today . . . nor would it be home tomorrow, she thought with a tinge of sadness.

"I didn't know soldiers had to work," Christy said in surprise. "I thought they just marched and waved flags and shot off cannon."

"Well, silly!" Martin felt wise. "Marching and shooting is soldiers' work."

"Soldiers do important work," Nola said. "They keep the peace if they can and fight the wars if they must—" She stopped listening mentally to what she had just said. If Tom's work was so important, he had to put it first in his life. Was she furious with him because he didn't make her happiness and contentment his first concern? Or was he leaving all that to her, believing she could handle it herself? Like a lot of other things, it was puzzling. Maybe there should be easy answers, but there were not.

She sipped her coffee and watched the children eat her breakfast. Mama was probably right, she thought. She did need time to think, time to "get her emotions under control" as Mama had said. But as she dressed after the children had gone off with the lightened tray, she kept her thoughts away from Bitter Lake. Maybe she wasn't ready to place the blame honestly.

When Fannie called her to the phone, it was, astonishingly, the Colonel's Lady on the other end of the line. "Nola?" the crisp voice asked. "I was very surprised when I learned that you had left so suddenly. If anything I said to you caused you to make such an unwise decision, I hope you will reconsider. And come back home where you belong."

Nola caught her breath. "That's the most unapologetic apology I ever heard!"

"I didn't intend it for one," the Colonel's Lady said

blandly. "Why should I apologize? I simply told you some things you needed to know. I expected you to be mature enough to take constructive criticism."

"It wasn't you altogether," Nola said truthfully. "It was Tom agreeing with you. Against me."

"There's another thing," said the Colonel's Lady. "You should not have phoned Tom to force him to share your anger. You do not *ever* send your husband out on duty with a divided mind. You must not claim any part of his attention for your little problems—"

"*Little!* When you nearly ate me alive!"

"—absurd little problems when he needs all his concentration for his own safety and that of the men under his command. You understand me?"

Nola found herself nodding mutely at the telephone.

The Colonel's Lady apparently expected no audible answer. She went on. "I do realize there is much for a service bride to learn, but many of us are willing to teach you. You have many good qualities, and I'm sure you love Tom dearly, which makes a good beginning. It will probably be a good thing for you to spend a few days with your family. Then come back, and we'll get on with making you into as good a wife as dear Tom deserves. Good-bye now."

Nola stood staring at the receiver in her hand long after the click had terminated Maggie Slayton's monologue. She was still staring when Julie came in and, taking the receiver from her sister, cradled it.

"Come on down to the courtyard," Julie said. "Mama

and Pa want to have coffee with you." As they went downstairs, she added, "I picked up the extension and naturally couldn't put it down again. She kind of laced into you but actually she didn't sound so bad."

"No, she isn't," Nola said to her own surprise. "You could like her if she wasn't always right. What she thinks the wives ought to do is really what they should do. Maybe I just don't very much want to be a service wife."

Julie stood with one foot reaching for the next step. "Did you say what I thought you said?"

"I only want to be Tom's wife. I know I tore up the earth to make him marry me before he was really ready. I do love him very much. But I didn't promise to love the service! Or honor a forsaken post in the middle of nowhere! And I surely didn't promise to obey the Colonel's Lady!"

They were in the courtyard by that time. Julie took up the shears kept at hand in her mother's garden basket and began trimming the lemon thyme. It was an unending task that was a therapy. The herb grew between the paving blocks so vigorously that by the time one end of the courtyard was groomed the other end needed cutting again. To shear the clean-smelling plants to tidy mats scented the hand and soothed the mind.

Julie handed Nola a few sprigs and went on with the cutting. "You look as if your nerves need calming."

Nola sniffed obediently, then threw the thyme down.

107

"Oh, *you*! If Tom would resign and come back to the city, he could pilot something for Pa. Then we could live in a civilized place. That isn't too much to ask, is it?"

"Only you and Tom know what is too much or not enough."

"Where is everybody?" Nola demanded. "Didn't you say Mama and Pa wanted me? If they're going to lay me out, I'd just as soon get it over with." She bent to pick up the sprigs of thyme, rolling them in her hand and then sniffing the lemony odor. "I want to phone Tom— No, I'll wait until he comes off duty. The Colonel's Lady doesn't approve of phone calls that might distract her officers."

Pa and Mama came then. Taking her cup from the tray her father offered, Nola said, "Could we have my scolding first?"

Gerald Foret dropped into his chair and smiled at his daughter ferociously. "Let me begin by saying that, if your mother had agreed, I wouldn't have let you in the house last night. I'd have put you on a plane back to Bitter Lake so fast your silly head would still be spinning."

Nola was hurt. "This is my home, Pa! Can't I come home?"

Gerald was firm in disputing her. "This *was* your home. Your home *now* is with your husband."

"Now, Gerald," Mama said. "I'm sure Nola realizes that. She knows too that she is always welcome here."

"You said it, Louise. I didn't." Gerald Foret started a gesture with his coffee cup, then righted it. "Nola is not welcome to run back here and snuggle down in a nice soft nest of self-pity every time she has a quarrel with her husband. I won't have it, Louise!"

"Now, Gerald. You know very well newlyweds have these wrinkles to iron out. It's our duty as parents to help them adjust to each other. To help in every way we can."

"Well, what are these wrinkles we have to help you smooth?" he asked Nola. "You don't like the place where you have to live? And some of the people you must live with ruffle your feathers, huh?"

Nola said nothing. The way Pa put it her problems did seem trivial . . . almost as little and absurd as Maggie Slayton had called them.

Pa was still talking. "As an officer's wife, you'll be living in places that will make Bitter Lake look like an anteroom to Paradise. And the older you get, the longer the list of people you could do without."

Nola was goaded into answering that: "If Tom should resign, we could come back here to live. You could find a place for him at the airline, couldn't you, Pa? You're always hiring pilots."

"Just one minute. Think about Tom instead of yourself for a change. How would you like it if your in-laws busily and sweetly pressured you into something you didn't want?"

"It would be for Tom's good."

"Says who? I doubt that Tom wants to give up the career he's been educated and trained to pursue. Even for you, sweetie. Or he's not half the man I think he is."

Nola sighed. No use trying to argue with Pa when he was riding a high horse. Like now. "Nothing is working out the way I thought it would! I only wanted—oh, I don't know! Maybe I wanted things to stay the way they were. Maybe I don't even know what I want!"

"I think that's entirely possible," Louise said, breaking her silence. "So it's time for you to stop and think about it. What do you want?"

Nola was outraged. "I expected you to see my side, Mama!"

"Oh, I do. But that doesn't blind me to the fact that yours is the wrong side now," Louise said tartly. "You don't really want things to stay the way they are, dear. If you do, you're fighting change, and that's an old person's battle. The young, like you and Tom, should thrive on change. What's so great about having today just like yesterday and a carbon copy of tomorrow? I'm sure that one reason you fell so in love with Tom was because you wanted a change, and he was certainly something different. You were a little bored with all this—" Louise's gesture took in the house, the family, the university, the city. "You wanted a change even if you didn't know it."

Pa took the floor again. "You have to remember that a marriage takes time. Time for you and Tom to grow up to what you expect of each other. If each of you expects different things from marriage, then you must make your expectations match up. What each of you wants depends upon your past and your hopes for the future. You have to remember that Tom has a past and dreams all his own as well as you do."

Nola bristled at all the criticism. "Why does the girl always have to give in? What's so bad about doing, being, living, working the way *she* wants it?"

"A man has a right to decide where and how he will make a living. He's a fool if he lets his wife tell him how to live his life," Pa said bluntly. "If he gives up his real ambitions and annexes himself to her, he diminishes them both. In the end, she loses more than he does."

There was silence in the courtyard, broken only by the *snick* of the shears in Julie's hands. Then Louise handed her cup to Gerald to place on the tray and went to take Nola's face between her hands.

"Sweetie, don't worry about fairness. The one who gives the most gets the most. Give and take in marriage can't be equal, or you'd hang up on dead center. One of you must give a little more than the fair share. It doesn't have to be the same one who is generous every time. Give and take; that way the marriage can move ahead."

Nola saw the look her father and mother exchanged. It confirmed what she had always known, that they loved each other devotedly within the framework of a good marriage. She would have to listen to them, even when they lectured as tiresomely as now, for they knew.

"You'll have to decide for yourself, Nola," her father said seriously as if he had known what she was thinking.

Louise kissed her daughter. "And you must be sure."

That word again. Sure . . . sure . . . sure . . . The sound of it was sobering.

nine ❧❧❧❧

YOU DON'T KEEP BOOKS WITH LOVE

The day moved slowly. Nola wandered around the house, talked with Mama and Julie when she encountered them, played with Christy and Martin . . . all with an eye on the clock. As soon as Tom could be expected back at the quarters, she would call him.

When she thought it was time, she sat looking at the phone, planning what she would say. First she would forgive Tom sweetly for the heartless way he had treated her when she had been so upset by the Colonel's Lady. Then she would persuade him to come here for a few days' visit. Surely he had a few days' leave coming to him? When he came, she would try every persuasion to get him to decide to live here. He would see how much better everything would be. But that was for later. She lifted the receiver and began to dial.

The phone rang and rang. Tom might not have come straight home . . . maybe he was in the shower. . . . He answered then. "Quarters. Captain Cartright here."

Nola couldn't speak for a moment. This was what having your heart in your throat meant. She tried again. ". . . Tom?"

"Oh, Nola? Hello . . ."

"Tom, forgive me for running off. You found my note?"

"Yes, I found it."

"You said at breakfast I could go home to visit for a little while—"

"I don't remember it like that, honey."

"Well, you didn't say I *couldn't* go! But I wouldn't have gone if you hadn't agreed with the Colonel's Lady. Tom, she was cold and sarcastic and . . . and hateful! But let's don't talk about her now. Tom, do you have some leave? Could you come here for a few

114

days? Then we could go back to Bitter Lake together."

To her dismay Nola heard doubt in his voice. Tom didn't answer with the bright sureness she loved. His refusal sounded restrained. They weren't getting through to each other, she thought in panic.

"No, I can't come just now. There's something— Why don't you stay and get your visit out? Then when you want to come back . . ." His voice trailed away.

Suddenly Nola was angry. "I suppose you'll meet me at the airport with a band! Maybe I won't come back! No one in her right mind would live in Bitter Lake by choice!"

"What did you expect, Nola? You knew I was an Air Force officer when you married me. Wasn't it obvious that we'd live at an Air Force base?"

"I didn't expect wind and sand whistling and crackling around our dear little substandard home and the rundown officers' club! Tom, do you have to stay in service?"

His answer was carefully patient. "Honey, I come from a service family. My father, my grandfather, my brother. I've been educated by my country, at considerable expense, to be an officer. Matter of fact, I've never wanted to be anything else. I suppose I could resign—"

She interrupted eagerly. "Oh, Tom, that would solve everything!"

He ignored the interruption. "—but I don't intend to."

"Oh, Tom, I can't bear it! *Why* do you have to be a soldier! I try to keep from thinking about the awfulness of the war, but no matter how I try, I can't push it down out of sight!"

"And right now I tell you—stop trying!" Tom's voice was stern. "It's the final insult to the men who are bleeding out there that the people they're dying for can't make themselves uncomfortable by so much as giving that suffering a thought! Don't you ever say such a thing to me again."

Nola caught her breath. "Oh, Tom, I can't bear to have you talk to me like this. . . ."

"Then don't think like that. Look, honey. I'm no braver than the next guy. I'm not a bit anxious to get killed for my country or for any other reason. I'd like to keep on living with you for years to come . . . if you shape up a little. But the war isn't the only way you can lose your life. You can get it going down to the corner to buy a pack of cigarettes and maybe just as sure if you smoke 'em. So the way I see it, you can die for nothing, or you can die for something."

Tom's voice dropped then. He was no longer shouting into the phone as he went on: "I'm not sayng this war is *all* right. But neither is it *all* wrong. What I can't stand is a picture of myself as I'd look if I sat here on top of the greatest wealth, the greatest security, the greatest ease the world has ever known and did nothing. Mind you, I haven't had a thing to do with piling up that wealth and security and ease. It's built

116

on the sweat and responsibility of all the people who went before me. All I've done is be here to inherit. So who am I to hog it all for myself? Why can't I spare a little to make other lives richer and safer? I don't have to decide whether the world is going to hell or not. Even if it is, I'd rather be the fellow that helped put on the brakes than the one that gave Mother Earth a shove."

There was a long silence before he went on. "I suppose I could be content and reasonably useful as an engineer or a commercial pilot. But how long would that satisfy you, Nola? You'd balk—the way you look at things now—at the moving around an engineer almost has to do if he gets ahead at his profession. And I'd be away half the time as a commercial pilot."

"There's something wrong with everything, isn't there?" Nola asked forlornly. She had had to try twice before even those words would come out.

"Very true." Tom's voice was brisk and everyday again. "I tell you *what*, Little Wife—" He laughed a a little. "As a matter of fact, that's what I've been doing! You stay there and think things over for a few days and let me know when you reach some conclusions. 'Bye now."

Nola heard a click and the empty hum of the line. Tom hadn't said he loved her or missed her or even that he wanted her back. He hadn't let her explain really. He wasn't ready to be forgiven. She slammed down the receiver, but that was futile too, for there was no one on the other end of the line to have his ear affronted. She ran upstairs hoping to get into her room before any one saw the tears that blinded her.

She didn't stay hidden in her room for long. Her rage soon dried her tears, and her pride compelled her to act as if all were right with her matrimonial world. She wouldn't give Tom the satisfaction of knowing that his attitude grieved her . . . not that he was likely to know one way or another. He didn't write, so Nola didn't either. A few more unsatisfactory phone calls and then days stretched between them, arid and silent.

Nola plunged into a feverish round of dinners and parties. On her birthday Alcee Sonnier, her godfather, arranged a select and fussy affair for her that would, he promised, get her back into the social activity of her circle of friends.

"I assume that you do want back," he told Nola, his bright black eyes searching her face to see what it would add to what he had already guessed. "I rather think there has been a slight rift in the lute, has there not? Or should I say, the honeymoon seems to be over? Never mind, you don't need to answer. I can peep through a grindstone as soon as most. So there's all the more reason for you to go out and be seen. You can't sit at home and pine away."

So Nola went out, often escorted by Freddy Hefner, who pried as persistently as Mr. Sonnier. He didn't ask her point-blank if she were home to stay. He got
118

around it by wanting to know if she would be in the city long enough to take a part in the play that would soon go into production.

"There's a lovely role for you, Nola darling," he coaxed. "But I'd have to know that you'd be here long enough to appear in it."

He waited hopefully but Nola didn't answer. She was thinking that Freddy sounded more than a little precious.

At Mr. Sonnier's perfectly appointed table, she found herself wondering if "gracious living" couldn't be overdone. The delicate old china and silver, set out on a damask cloth worn thin by years of use, was beautiful. So was the centerpiece of garden flowers. But Mr. Sonnier had a not-quite-hot-enough plate exchanged, and he sent the salad bowl back twice for a delicate change in its herb content. It was too much fussing even for the confirmed male-spinster he had become.

The dinner-table conversation bothered Nola too. There was much laughter, for much of the slightly malicious talk and bits of gossip were amusing. But the subjects seldom strayed from a small, tight enclave of intimates. The group of friends seated at the antique table eating delicious food suddenly seemed to Nola too ingrown, a bit insensitive, more than a little smug.

"No," she said finally to Freddy, "I won't be here long enough to take the part. I don't know exactly when I'll be leaving, but I can't be in your play."

One afternoon she let herself into the courtyard limp with the steamy heat and hotter still with exasperation. The gate had recently been oiled and the thick carpet of thyme muffled her footsteps so she heard her mother talking.

"I don't understand Nola at all," her mother was saying. "When she first came home, she seemed so glad to be with us again, delighted with everything, so glad to see her friends. In fact I thought she was settling back nicely into her place as a daughter in the house. Now it is all changed. She's critical of everyone and everything, so restless and dissatisfied. At times, Gerald, she's downright peevish."

"You were wrong in opposing me when I said she should go back to a job in the terminal. Would have done her a lot of good."

Martin and Christy came whooping down the courtyard from the back of the house, swinging the lariats Nola had bought for them when she changed planes at Dallas. One cast made with more enthusiasm than accuracy whacked her sharply on the head.

"Oh, for heaven's sake!" she said crossly. "Can't a person walk through a gate without getting her head knocked off!"

"Oh, Sister, we're sorry," Christy and Martin said. "We've been trying to be extra nice to you too. Because Papa told us you have something on your mind. Where is it? We can't see it."

"Oh, *you!* Go see if you can lasso Faimie's cat." Nola
120

shooed them away, sure that the experienced old pet would be in no danger.

She walked into the living room then to confront her parents and Julie. "I heard what you said about me, Mama. And you too, Pa! And I know what you were getting ready to say, Julie! And it kills me to admit it, but you are all three right."

Tears rolled down Nola's cheeks, and her words poured out as helplessly. "Instead of being with Tom while I can, what have I done? Sat around here being a nuisance! Gone out with people I don't care about. Gone to stupid parties. Tried to convince myself I was having fun, fun, fun!" She stopped for breath, then ran on. "Like this afternoon. I sat for four hours at a bridge table with this girdle killing me—" She broke off to wail, "I've gained five pounds on party food! —and trying to remember all the conventions so Mr. Sonnier wouldn't tut-tut me. I can just see myself going on at more bridge tables, with more party food, making the same mistakes with different partners!"

Julie was puzzled. "I thought you were playing with Mama's foursome today because she had a headache. Why was Mr. Sonnier there?"

"Aunt Amina sent Mr. Sonnier to play in her place the way Mama sent me. And he's a hair-splitting he-spinster! I don't care if he is my godfather and I ought to respect his years. Mama, he went over every hand *three* times. *I've* got to improve my game, he says, because there's nothing like playing a good game to

121

prepare you for a lively old age. The Colonel's Lady was a shark at the table, but I'll take her over Mr. Sonnier any day—"

Over Nola's outburst the others exchanged looks. Julie sprang to her feet hoping she wouldn't laugh out loud. The situation wasn't funny, but the way Mama maneuvered Nola was. She turned her sister toward the stairs.

"Come on. I'll help you pack. You won't have time to get more than one bag ready, but I'll send the rest of your things."

Nola choked on a sob. "What things? Pack what?"

"There's a plane for Bitter Lake in an hour," Julie said. "As I see it, you've got a choice between Mr. Sonnier and the Colonel's Lady, and you just said you'd chose her over him. Besides, with her you get Tom."

Nola stared at her sister, then turned to look at her parents. As they watched her, her face began to come alive. The peevish dissatisfaction went away and was replaced with hope and love and something else that her family had never seen in Nola's face before.

"Just being together, that's all," she said slowly. "I knew that in the beginning, but I got sidetracked. You don't keep books on marriage. You don't count up to see who gets most or who gives most—"

She started for the stairs, then ran back to kiss Mama and Pa. "Thank you. Thank you both for whatever you did to open my stupid eyes." Then she took the stairs two at a time with Julie following.

She snatched a bag from the clothes closet, then stood in the middle of the floor holding it. She said in a wondering voice, "I saw inside my silly head this afternoon, Julie! I did. I looked at my marriage and understood that I had been seeing only the surface. I'd expected that surface to be smooth as a mirror so it could reflect back to me my irresistible self! I really believed Tom and I would share only pleasant things. Year after year he and I would go out to dinners and dances, always dressed to the teeth, making clever small talk, always on our best behavior with each other, each of us determined always to please."

"Sweetie—" Julie shook her sister's arm gently. "You don't want to miss that plane."

"I don't! I won't! I've broken that foolish mirror, Julie. It doesn't have to reflect impossible perfection or perfect happiness. It can show pain and disappointment and disagreement . . . Tom when he needs a slave . . . me with my hair in a mess. Me when I'm being unreasonable and Tom when he's infuriating. Oh, he can make me so mad! Just wait until I see him again!"

The tears were still wet on Nola's cheeks, but her eyes sparkled and her laughter joined Julie's. She ran to the clothes closet and began snatching hangers.

She brought the armful of clothes to the bed where Julie had opened a bag. "Just wait until I see the Colonel's Lady again! I'll apologize and make her think

NOW FOR NOLA

I'm Judy O'Grady and her sister under the skin if it kills us both!"

Then Julie understood the change in her sister's face. Now under her mischievous laughter Nola looked grown-up.

ten ❦❦❦❦

YOU CAN GET TIRED OF
HOLDING HANDS

Nola watched the airport runways spray out ahead as
the plane approached for its landing. Afternoon sun
winked from the windows of the buildings and turned
the silvery skin of the plane taking off below them to
a blinding flash. Although she could not see its mark-

ing, she knew it because of the timing. Trans West flights to and from the city passed each other here with only a few minutes difference. As Nola's plane landed, the other climbed to its flight altitude.

Coming down the steps, she scanned the uplifted seeking faces, the waving welcoming hands, sure she would see Tom at once. She had sent a telegram before she left the city. So he must be late— Maybe he was in the field, and they couldn't deliver the message. Nola felt a growing panic. Tom's face was not there smiling in welcome; his hand was not waving.

Nola searched through the lounges, looked into the coffee shop. She went back through the corridors she had already traversed. Tom wasn't in the airport. She hurried out to the parking area and searched up and down the rows of cars. Tom's car wasn't there either.

At last she went back into the coffee shop and carried her cup to a table in the farthest corner. It was puzzling. If Tom couldn't come to meet her himself, surely he could have sent someone. She hadn't gone to the information desk. The message was probably there. She hurried out, leaving her coffee to get cold.

No message there for Mrs. Tom Cartright. She hesitated a moment, then shook her head at the clerk's offer of further help. "No thank you, there's nothing you can do." Probably nothing anyone can do, she added silently. Tom didn't want her back.

She walked slowly back to the coffee bar and bought another cup. Sitting down at the table in the farthest corner, she looked with bewilderment at the two cups, one hot, one cold before her.

She was still staring at the cups when Fran Bishop came. "Nola! It is you. I couldn't believe I saw you leaving the information desk. When did you come?"

"Oh, Fran . . . just now. Silly of me, but I expected to be met." Nola looked up at her friend. "Are you the official greeter?"

"The replacements unit left this morning," Fran said in a puzzled voice. "Why didn't you come either earlier or later? Oh," she said. "You didn't know."

She sat down in the chair opposite, and the two girls looked at each other without words. Nola resumed the aimless stirring of the coffee gone cold again. She lifted the cup to her lips, and held it without tasting. After a time Fran reached across the table and gently took the cup from Nola's hands.

"Don't tell me anything you don't want to," she said. "But there are times—and this is one of them—when I'd love to knock some husbands' heads together!"

Nola came to Tom's defense. "He probably wrote me. I didn't decide to come until a few hours ago. I guess my telegram couldn't be delivered."

"I heard your phone ringing and ringing," Fran said. "Then I saw the telegram in your box when I went to pick up our mail. So I called the Colonel's Lady, and she said to go ahead and open it. Then I came on to the airport, but I'm always late."

Nola picked up her bag and slid out of the bench.

127

"Thank you for coming, Fran. Could we go home now? I'll have to get my luggage."

"You can spend the night with us," Fran was saying. "You can't get back until tomorrow, for the plane for the city left just before yours came in. Tomorrow I'll help you pack."

Nola was shaking her head. "I mean home to our house."

"Stay alone in your quarters? Well, I can run over to sleep, so you wouldn't—"

Nola kept on shaking her head. "No, Fran, but thanks. I'll be all right. Better, in fact."

If she could be in her own place, she could decide what to do, Nola thought. A doubt flickered in the corner of her mind. What was there to do except go home again? Home? Where? Her real home was here at Bitter Lake. To go back to Mama and Papa was to leave home.

Life was like the game of musical chairs you played at kid parties. Prance around gaily until the music stopped. Then scramble to sit down. But your chair had been taken away, and there was no place for you.

"I'll be all right," she repeated. "With you and Dick next door— No, he's gone too, isn't he?"

Fran nodded soberly. "This class was trained for replacement duty in Vietnam. The colonel was assigned with them.

"The colonel that she is the lady of?"

"You could say that. Well, Tom had finished all the

simulated rescue operations possible here. So he wanted battlefield conditions to test the helicopter shield under fire."

"He didn't have to go," Nola said forlornly as she got into Fran's car. She wept as they drove out of the parking area.

Not looking away from her driving, Fran patted Nola's knee. "Don't take on, honey. There isn't much to please yourself in the service. Maybe Tom didn't have to go, but I'd say he *needed* to go. When you put as much of yourself into something as he has in that 'copter shielding, wouldn't you want to be the one to see it finished? Sure you would. So mop your eyes and don't be a baby, Baby."

Fran's matter-of-factness more than her own belief that Fran was right dried Nola's tears. "If I could believe that," she said slowly.

"Well, try hard!" Fran laughed a little and patted Nola's knee again. "You take it too big, Nola. I doubt that you're having more newlywed trouble than usual."

"Our quarrels are unimportant?"

Fran was sure of it. "All brides go through the same routine. I know I did. They believe that old chestnut, 'All for love and the world well lost.' Phooey! So the bride wants to turn the lights low and sit in lover's lap all evening like in their courting days. What's the sense of that? the groom asks, when you can go to bed together with the blessing of church and state. You can get tired of holding hands and mooning into each

129

others' eyes. Especially if there's a good game on TV. A man has to earn a living, so no matter how much he loves you, he can't spend all his time and energy on you. He has to do his best with his job, see? So a smart little wife doesn't fight the job—or the office or the boss or especially the boss' wife."

"For boss' wife, read the Colonel's Lady," said Nola.

"You get the message."

They were silent as Fran turned into the cloverleaf that left the highway and turned them toward the base. At the gates Nola thought the guard eyed her in some surprise and was sure of it when Fran said after they drove through, "Don't mind the gawkers."

"You mean people are talking about Tom and me?"

"Naturally. Nothing is secret on a base. Out here in the boondocks we have to make our own amusements."

"Oh, Fran! Don't be so cynical."

"Realistic is the word, dear. Which reminds me that the smartest thing you can do is call the Colonel's Lady and make an early appointment for an abject apology."

"Do I have to?"

"No, but you'll be very sorry if you don't."

"Just wait until I get my hands on Tom Cartright!" Nola said fiercely. "The things I have to do because of him!"

Fran laughed and after a little Nola could see it was funny too.

But the laughter didn't prepare Nola for the closed

130

and silent quarters that had housed her honeymoon dreams. Fran helped her turn on the air conditioner, then left, having exacted a promise to come over if she felt the least uneasy.

Nola laid the door key on the table that was a packing box under its brave new skirt and took out the steak bundled in dry ice that she had brought in her luggage. She put the beef that had been designed for a reunion dinner in the freezer. When Tom came back, it would be waiting for him.

In the morning she would see the Colonel's Lady and make her apologies. Now that she wasn't going to live at the base, it wouldn't be actually necessary to make peace with that formidable iron hand in the velvet glove, but she was sorry that she had shirked her responsibilities. For Tom's sake she could swallow what rags of pride were left to her. Not many of them . . . not with the whole installation whispering and wondering about her private life.

She walked restlessly back and forth through the house. Tom had left everything very clean and uncluttered. The living room where she had worked so hard to overcome the handicap of those red, red walls looked good now, she conceded. The slipcovers of blue and white mattress ticking she had sewed so poorly and the "rug" she had painted on the floor made a good effect. The packing boxes upholstered into cube tables, the mop-handle curtain poles . . . Nola looked on her work and found it not too bad.

131

In the kitchen she set the shining copper kettle on to boil. Mama thought a good hot cup of tea was the answer to most problems. Nola needed an answer. Looking at the cabinets decorated with flowers and vegetables cut from seed packets, she thought that was one of her better ideas. So were the curtains she had contrived from dyed and knotted cotton cord.

In the bedroom her hands automatically smoothed and tucked the spread and plumped the pillows. With all the will in the world a man couldn't make a bed right. Oh, maybe a camp bed. They were always bragging, those men, about blankets stretched so tightly a coin would bounce on them, but they couldn't do much with a real bed.

It wasn't the curtains or the spread or the bedside table made from half a packing box covered with contact paper that made this room so poignant. It was the heart and center of the life she and Tom had begun together here, the lovemaking, the talking in the intimate dark, the discoveries they had made about each other, finding another trait until then unknown, a different aspect of personality. Especially the wonder of seeing through another's eyes something not understood before . . . even the small disagreements . . . until this last and large one.

She spoke aloud to the girl in the mirror, "Maybe that's what the 'battle of the sexes' is all about. You," she said scornfully to her reflection, "think love is all of life, the beginning and the ending and the answer

132

to everything. But a man knows better. Maybe you can make him agree with you for a while, at least until the honeymoon is over. Then off he goes to build a helicopter shield and fight a war. And, poor silly girl-he-left-behind-him . . . you get furious!"

From the kitchen the boiling kettle whistled loudly and, Nola felt, derisively.

Because she took so long to get to sleep on her dampened pillow, Nola was late waking next morning. She stared at her watch in consternation, but it agreed with the clock. By this time she had thought to have her apology to the Colonel's Lady behind her and be in town ready to take the morning flight back to the city.

The pantry provided coffee and little else for breakfast, so there was no reason to linger over it. Nola washed her cup and saucer, emptied the coffeepot and made the bed. Now she had removed all traces of her overnight stay in the little house. How could she pass the time until the afternoon plane? If she stayed here, the Colonel's Lady was sure to come. Of course she knew of Nola's return. Fran had said, and Nola believed it, that everything was known to every body on the base. So she would prefer to apologize to Maggie Slayton in some private place if she could find one.

Oh, Dottie. Dottie Harper. She hadn't called Dottie before her impulsive dash for the city. Nola tied a scarf

133

over her head against the everlasting wind of these wide open places and picked up her handbag. She had gone out on the small porch and closed the door before she noticed the mist of falling rain and remembered she had no car. She would have to go in again and hope the Colonel's Lady wouldn't come out in damp weather.

Only she couldn't get in. The key was locked inside. In her mind's eye Nola could see it on the skirted table made from a packing box where she had laid it when she came in yesterday. She'd go next door to Fran's— no, today was Thursday, Fran's morning at the thrift shop. So she would walk over to Dottie's.

Nola set off down the road behind the quarters with a purposeful air. No use parading her stupidity to any of the other wives. "Walk as if you're thinking of your figure," she told herself. The wives were nice girls, but new bride that she had been—and blind besides, she added now—she hadn't tried very hard to make friends. She promised herself that would be the first thing she'd do now.

She had gone only a little way down the road before she regretted her plan. Her shoes collected small stones, and once she turned an ankle stepping into a sand-masked hollow. Walking on the edge was little better. No cool green carpet there. The sparse tufts of grass snagged her stockings with spiny animosity. The equally sparse low bushes threatened her with vari-sized thorns.

Homesickness overwhelmed Nola as she thought of the courtyard in the city. There the banana plants grew next to the moss-grown wall, and the lemon thyme perfumed the still hot air. Nothing like that greenness or perfume here . . . or was there?

Looking closely, she found surprising similarities. Washed by the gentle mist of rain, a clump of cactus glowed with the same tender green of the banana leaves. The texture of the cactus flowers was as thin and golden and silken as the sunlight. Some scraggly olive-brown bushes looked as if each small leaf had been newly polished, and when she bent to examine them more closely, she caught a delicate scent. She broke off a twig and rubbed the leaves between her palms to strengthen the odor. It was familiar and somehow remindful of city streets. Then she had it. The smell of tar and creosote and hot asphalt. Imagine . . .

Her spirits lifting as she went, Nola walked faster. The large armored bug that threatened her with upraised claws and a strong vinegarish smell was a caricature, not a danger. When a big, crested, clownish bird raced across the road to dive under the lacy thorns of a mesquite, she called good morning to it. The bird emerged and ran on up the road, head turned over his shoulder in curiosity. He seemed friendly enough, Nola thought, but was plainly crazy too, or he wouldn't be running down the road in the rain with her.

If she had been driving, she wouldn't have noticed so much. The cactus and the bushes would have been only scraggly nondescript vegetation, the bird only a flicker of motion. She wouldn't have seen the thousand variations of bronze and gold and green that, brightened by the moisture in the air, clothed the hills with beauty.

Nola remembered something Tom had said. How did it go? That everything evened out, that the good posts had some drawbacks and the bad posts had good points. If you looked, there was beauty and many things of interest. "Why, you dear little Pollyanna!" Nola said mockingly to herself.

Dottie opening her door to Nola's knock seemed neither overly surprised nor overly welcoming. "Oh. . . . How are you, Nola? Come in. You'll have to excuse the mess. I have to leave the house until later. I'm trying to get the baby ready to take over to the nursery when I go to the ACS coffee."

Nola hesitated. "Maybe I'd better not stop if you're going out soon."

"Oh, no, come in. You can visit with me until I have to go." A sudden curiosity showed on Dottie's face. "When did you come back? Sit down and tell me how things were back home. You went off in *such* a hurry."

Nola didn't want to talk about it. What was the use if everyone on the base knew all about her private life already?

"Oh, not really in a hurry. What's this bunch-of-letters coffee you're going to? I wonder why the service

136

must call everything a lot of letters you can't pro-
nounce?"

"ACS? You ought to know about Army Community
Service," Dottie said in a faintly chiding voice. "I don't
know what I'd have done without it. How come you
don't know? Didn't someone ask you to a Welcome
Strangers meeting?"

"That does ring a bell . . . faintly," Nola remembered. "When we first came, I was invited to several
different dos, but I was too busy to go."

Dottie whistled. "No wonder you got in bad with
the lady brass. Let me tell you, dear. In our situation
here, invitation equals command, and you'd better
believe it. Unless you're having a baby or the house
is on fire, you'd better go."

"You have to be putting me on."

"I'm not," Dottie insisted. "You should have gone
to the first whatever-it-was you were invited to. One
of the main purposes of ACS is to welcome newcomers
and brief them on the base programs."

Nola sighed. "I could have used some briefing. So I
goofed."

"Yes, you did," Dottie said candidly. "Here—" She
thrust the baby, full of formula and sweetly sleepy, into
Nola's arms. "Hold him while I get dressed, will you?
Come sit on the bed so we can talk." She went on.
"Honestly, Nola, I blame Tom for most of this. Oh, you
weren't too bright! But he should have told you the

137

facts of service life. ACS has a good family-counseling service."

Nola looked blank. "What would we want with that?"

"You have to be kidding," Dottie said loudly above the noise of the bathroom faucets. "The walls in quarters not only have ears—they have tongues to spread the news."

"So Tom and I had a few disagreements."

"The way I heard it, Tom wouldn't have been so eager to put in for more time in Vietnam if you hadn't walked out on him."

"What! I walked out on him? Dottie, I only went home for a few days." In her agitation Nola clutched the baby until he whimpered.

"*Don't* wake him—" Dottie came hopping, stepping into her shoes as she came to take the baby from Nola. "I didn't mean to upset you, Nola. I just repeated what I was told. I'm sorry, but I do have to go now. This meeting is important. To me anyway. It's for the wives of men overseas. You ought to go too."

Nola shook her head. "I don't think so. I'll go back home—" She remembered the locked-in key then and told Dottie about it.

"You can take mine," Dottie said. "Just leave it in your door, and I'll pick it up sometime. I'll borrow Molly's when I come home. Any key here fits any door, didn't you know that? I planned to walk over to the
138

club. It's just a step. But I could ask Molly to run you back to your house."

"No, I want to walk," Nola said. "It's stopped raining now. Thanks, Dottie, and I'll see you."

A little later fitting the "any" key into the "any" lock, Nola thought she had been stupidly self-engrossed. She turned the key wondering if there was a kind of symbolism in the act.

eleven

A BETTER WIFE

The phone rang inside the house. *Tom!* Nola tried the
key upside down, then dropped it in her frantic haste.
Unlocked finally and thrown wide, the door bounced
against the wall as she snatched at the phone.

"Hello . . . hello! Oh . . . Mama. Yes, I'm all
right. . . ."

Nola had forgotten to call last night as she had promised to do. "I'm sorry, Mama, but I was late getting out here and . . ."

It wasn't the fact that she hadn't called that had alarmed her mother. Mama—this with some asperity—was accustomed to forgetful, inconsiderate children. But when an airmail special delivery letter mailed from the West Coast had come for Nola, Mama was understandably confused. Hadn't Nola gone to Bitter Lake to be with Tom? Then where was he? What was going on? Should she open the letter and read it over the phone?

Nola answered the last question first. Whatever might be in the letter, she wanted to read it for herself. "No, Mama, just forward it to me here."

She stopped abruptly. Now why had she said that? Why hadn't she told Mama to keep the letter there? Wasn't she going back to the city as soon as possible? Something in her mind spoke with complete conviction. *No, I'm not going back just now. Don't ask me why I'm not, because I don't know.*

That one answer wasn't going to satisfy Mama, so Nola went on. "This class of pilots was the last that will be trained here. Most of them were replacements assigned to Vietnam—"

Mama caught her breath in horror. "Tom has gone to Vietnam? You're alone there?"

"It was very sudden, and I'm sure Tom couldn't reach me. I imagine this letter will make it all clear."

141

Nola improvised but was not clear why she felt it necessary to do so.

Pa got on the phone back in the city. "Nola, you can't stay there alone. Pack up and come home. You hear me, child?"

Nola heard and wanted to obey that loving-father voice as much as she had ever wanted anything. If she could go home! If she could be nothing but Pa's child! Leaving behind all the necessity to make decisions, to know her own mind, to consult anyone's wishes except her own. How hard it was for the child inside to grow up! Passionately she wanted to be unreasonable and unreliable, selfish and self-centered again. Above all, she wanted to be able to blame someone beside herself for everything that went wrong!

So she was astonished to hear that inner conviction speaking with her own voice. "I can't come right now, Pa. Truly I can't, for a number of reasons. Don't worry about me. I'm all right. Lonely, but I'd miss Tom just as much back there. Tell Mama good night. I love you all. Good-bye, Pa. I'll be all right."

She cradled the phone slowly. "I'll be all right," she repeated aloud.

Behind her a voice said dryly, "I'm sure I hope so."

The Colonel's Lady sat on the slipcovered sofa. Maggie Slayton looked cool and well groomed from her smartly sleek, pepper-and-salt hair to her narrow, well-shod feet. Her blue eyes and her voice were equally cool.

142

"I mean that sincerely, Nola," she said. "I couldn't help overhearing your phone conversation. You had left the door open, and I'm sure you didn't expect me to stand outside in the damp. It's raining quite a little now. You were talking with your family, of course."

Nola nodded.

"Do sit down, my dear." The Colonel's Lady offered Nola a chair in her own house, then suggested that the open door be closed. Then what Nola considered to be an interrogation went on.

"You said you were *not* going home soon?" Maggie Slayton asked. "That's what I thought. You're making another mistake there, Nola. It would be better if you went back, probably to stay. Dear Tom does deserve a better wife."

Nola stared at her in a state of shock. How dare she! As a wife was she such a failure even this outsider could see it would be better for Tom if she left? Anger and hurt warred in her mind and on her face. The anger blazed into words.

"If Tom tells me that, maybe I'll believe it. What do you know about the way I feel? You with your calm, tranquil marriage, believing military routines are the only way to live! I don't suppose you ever doubt a thing you do or get depressed thinking about the things you don't! You've had time to get used to being alone. You probably don't even mind it, you . . . you iceberg!"

She might have gone on even more recklessly, but

before her eyes, the glacial, angry coldness of Maggie Slayton's face dissolved into a misery like her own. The cool blue eyes misted with tears, the proudly held head bent over her hands gripped in anguish.

"I almost wish I were like that . . . the way you describe me," the Colonel's Lady said brokenly. "Every time Wes leaves, I die a little. So sad and discouraged I can scarcely keep up with all the things he would want me to do, afraid to look into the future, so fearful that our luck will run out this time. . . ."

Nola swiped furiously at the angry tears that blurred her sight. She couldn't believe that voice was saying those words. Couldn't believe the Colonel's Lady was another distressed, forlorn wife—

On her knees before the older woman without really knowing how she got there, Nola caught the twisting hands in her own. "R-remember m-me, Colonel's Lady? I'm Judy O'Grady."

Maggie Slayton looked up with the ghost of a smile. Then she lifted Nola to sit beside her, and for a long time they wept together. Characteristically the Colonel's Lady recovered first. Nola was still gulping and sniffing when she began to hear the words that were offered her along with paper tissues.

"That's enough now," Maggie Slayton was saying with some of her usual briskness returning. "A good cry is fine, and it's done me a great deal of good. But we can't turn ourselves into sodden messes of self-

144

pity. Go wash your face, child. Then we can think what is best to do."

Astonishment cut Nola's sobs short. "D-do?" she stuttered. "What can I d-do but go back home?"

"Don't be stupid." The admonition was stern.

"S-stupid? Y-you said yourself Tom deserved a better wife!"

"Exactly. I didn't say that Tom deserved *another* wife, did I? That's what we must do. Find means of making you a better wife."

Nola finally began to laugh helplessly. "You make it s-sound so easy! And why do you care?"

"We always care about our wives, the colonel and I."

"Whether they want it or like it," Nola said pertly.

Maggie Slayton stiffened, then decided to laugh. "You are so terribly young. If you won't go wash your face, at least get some more tissues. Mine are all used up."

She got up then and headed for the kitchen. "What do you have to eat? I get breakfast early even when Wes isn't at home so I'm famished by this hour. I expected to snack a bit at the ACS coffee, but I came over here instead." She had noticed the seed-packet decoration on the cabinets. "Nola, that's very effective." She nodded in agreement with her thought. "You can do many things well."

Nola took her head out of the empty refrigerator.

"Oh, whatever I need to do, I suppose. I'm sorry. There isn't a thing except dry cheese and milk."

"Then get dressed, and we'll go over to that coffee even if it is late. I should be there anyway. The wives like Dottie Harper have such a problem."

"Dottie? I didn't so much as ask about Jack." Nola was appalled at her self-centeredness. "Has he been assigned to Vietnam too?"

"She no doubt thought you knew. You should have."

Nola was glum. "I should have known a lot of things."

"True. But you can learn, can't you?"

"I hope I can," Nola said more humbly than was usual. "Why does Dottie—and the other wives like her —have such a problem, Mrs. Slayton?"

"You may as well call me Maggie to my face," the Colonel's Lady said. "I know you all do when you speak of me among yourselves. About Dottie. Honestly, Nola! She's your friend, isn't she? Even for a bride, how can you be so self-centered?"

Nola wanted to say it had been easy, but didn't.

"Dottie doesn't have any place to go when she has to leave the base here. This installation is being phased out, but even if it were not, the wives can't stay on indefinitely in quarters after their husbands ship out."

"I didn't realize," Nola said.

The Colonel's Lady knew that. "Dottie doesn't have any family, and neither does Jack. She, like many of the wives, married right out of high school, so she

146

doesn't have any particular skills. She isn't trained for a job that would pay enough to rent much of an apartment or provide a sitter or nursery school for the baby. It will be hard for her to scrape by on her allowance if she doesn't work. And think how satisfying it would be if she could earn and save a nest egg? Career men must look ahead to retirement, when they'll need to buy a house or a business and will have to educate their children."

"I didn't realize," Nola said again. "Well, then, we'll have to help Dottie and the other wives who will have to move out too. Wouldn't you think somebody could match them up?"

"How do you mean?" The Colonel's Lady looked puzzled.

"This base being deactivated, with the quarters standing empty and the windows boarded up, while those wives have no place to go—"

Nola's eyes met the cool blue gaze of the Colonel's Lady. The idea grew instantly between them like a jinn bursting out of a bottle. Blue eyes and gray eyes began to blaze with excitement.

Nola thought out loud. "The first thing we should do is talk to Dottie. I mean, she's typical. What she thinks about the problem and any plan would be about what the other wives would think."

"What the Pentagon will do is more to the point." Maggie Slayton was practical.

Nola waved her hand in airy dismissal. "Tom says

the wives have more striking power than a wing of bombers. If they're organized, they'd be that much stronger—" Nola dashed for the bathroom. "I won't be a minute!"

The Colonel's Lady acknowledged Nola's sudden involvement with an amused lift of her eyebrows. While she waited, she inspected the ingenuities of Nola's interior decorating again with lifted brows and a smile.

When she emerged in a fresh dress with her curly hair smoothed, Nola said cheekily, "I washed. Do you want to see my ears?"

They chatted like old friends as Maggie Slayton drove down the road Nola had earlier traversed on foot. Approaching the corner near Dottie's house, Nola said, "Before we get to this coffee, could you tell me what those letters stand for? ACS?"

"Army Community Service. We give coffees every two months for the wives with husbands overseas. The girls have much the same problems and surely the same things to talk about. Off the base they often get the feeling that most civilians couldn't even find Vietnam on a map."

"If the war is over soon and the men come home," Nola began.

"Pray God it is," said the Colonel's Lady. "Pray God they do come home." They were silent for a moment. "Unless the millennium dawns tomorrow, servicemen will still go to hardship stations and service wives will need places to live while they wait here—"

148

A tinkling crash coming from Dottie's house interrupted her. Maggie Slayton braked the car to a stop, and they stared in that direction. A front window had been broken. Suddenly a shoe arced through the jagged opening and thumped to the steps. A book followed it.

"What in the world—" The Colonel's Lady reversed and turned, running her car close to the curb. "Come on, Nola. We have to check this!"

The door wasn't locked. When they opened it, they nearly fell over Dottie. She crouched on the floor, in tears, surrounded by sundry articles she had intended to throw through the window. When she saw them, she wept loudly.

"Oh, thank goodness! I thought no one would ever come," she wailed.

"What happened to you—never mind. Wait until we get you up—" Nola and the Colonel's Lady lifted Dottie to her feet. When one foot, noticeably swollen, touched the floor she yelped with pain and could barely hobble to a chair.

In the bedroom the baby cried steadily. Nola went to lift him from his crib, sopping wet and hiccuping with sobs. She cuddled him on her shoulder, patting and crooning. "There, there. . . . He's a poor mistreated boy. . . ."

"I went to pick Butch up," Dottie said. "After I gave you my key, Nola. And you had gone, walking back to your house. Thank goodness I *hadn't* picked him up. I stepped on a block he had thrown out of his crib and I fell so *hard*. I think I've broken my ankle." Dottie's voice trailed off in a wail.

Nola finished changing the baby. "It must have been uncomfortable in that puddle, which I don't think was all tears." She brought a bottle from the refrigerator and put him into the playpen. "There you go—" The baby's sobs changed to greedy sucking sounds.

"I couldn't reach the phone," Dottie was saying. "One or two cars went by, but I couldn't yell loud enough to make them hear me. Then I managed to scoot enough to gather up some stuff, and when I heard your car coming, I broke the window."

With their shoulders under her arms Dottie could hop to the car. When she had been painfully inserted in the back seat, the Colonel's Lady went back into the house to bring aspirin and water while Nola got the baby. Exhausted from crying and now full of comforting formula, he was asleep and didn't waken when shifted from playpen to his mother's arms.

Holding him close, Dottie closed her own eyes in the letdown of relief. "Suppose you hadn't come along and heard me! Suppose this had happened when I have to leave the quarters and find a place in town. If no one knew us, or knew I was missing from where I should be, or cared what became of us—"

"Take these." The Colonel's Lady offered the aspirin and the water to Dottie. "Somebody does care what becomes of you, so you can stop worrying. You aren't
150

going to have to find a place in town where no one knows you. That's a promise," she ended firmly.

The Colonel's Lady set down the empty glass and carefully closed Dottie in. In the driver's seat, she said to Nola, "Mark her down as one hundred percent in favor of our plan."

twelve 🌺🌸🌺🌸🌺

DEPENDENTS' DEPOT

It had begun with the look Nola and Maggie Slayton had exchanged over the empty refrigerator in the kitchen gay with seed-packet flowers and vegetables. It had progressed with nonstop talk. Tossing the idea back and forth, they had planned an ambitious pro-

152

gram before they got Dottie into the X-ray room at the base hospital.

"I can think of no good reason why my wives who have no place to go when their men ship out can't go on living here on the base," said the Colonel's Lady. "But hundreds of people will have to be convinced of the worth of the idea."

While they waited for Dottie to come out, they kept talking. "Look, Nola, you argue against everything so we can anticipate where opposition may come," the Colonel's Lady ordered.

"The base is going to shut down," Nola said.

"All the more room for wives and families. And it needn't shut down if we talk to the right people. If we go right to the top!"

"Who is 'we'?"

The Colonel's Lady was impatient. "You and I. Who else?"

"But I have to go home! I don't know if Tom and I will be able—"

"Nonsense. You can't go now. We have to make you over into the nice little wife Tom deserves. Besides I hate to write letters. I'll need you to do them for me."

"I wish Pa could hear you," Nola said admiringly. "That blasted secretarial course he made me take will turn out useful after all."

"We'll keep quoting, 'The service takes care of its own.' That's the Army Community Service slogan, you know. There are forty families at least with not much

153

place to go if they must leave here. Families with husbands and fathers doing a tour of duty in Vietnam, or Korea or Thailand, places where dependents can't follow. Think what it would mean to those women if they could have a good house, furnished if they needed it that way and with all utilities for something just over a hundred dollars a month." She waited.

Nola shook her head. "I can't find fault with that. I think it's great."

Maggie Slayton went on. "They could buy at the commissary and the post exchange. We can keep the thrift shop and the tideover service going too."

Nola shifted the baby in her lap and patted him into sounder sleep. "Nursery too. If the wives work, someone has to mind the younguns."

"They won't all work," the Colonel's Lady objected.

Nola took care of that. "Then the ones that don't work—outside their homes, that is—can take care of the children for the wives who do. Anyway, why can't we have job training? Something with real teeth? Ceramics and dressmaking and charm courses are dandy, but we need more. The wives who have skills should use them; the others could learn to earn. Then we'd need an employment service and job placing."

"Think BIG," the Colonel's Lady said dryly.

"I am," Nola said soberly. "Service wives need to be able and ready to take care of themselves and their families."

The Colonel's Lady looked sober too. "I know."

The fear for a husband's safety stood constantly at your shoulder, Nola thought. Dottie came out of X-ray then, pleased that she had no broken bones, but worried about instructions to stay off her badly sprained ankle.

"Nothing to it," Nola said. "I'll move in with you for a few days."

"Oh, Nola, *would* you? I've always hated to be alone. With Jack gone and no certainty that he will ever come back—"

"Now stop *that*," Nola said. "What will Butch think of you?"

"You are a darling," she told the baby at breakfast time next day. With the last pin fastened, she butted him with her head in a silly game that sent him into delighted giggles. "A perfect darling! And a perfect nuisance!"

Dottie struggled up in her bed. "Is it time to get up already? Gosh, why am I complaining? I've had the best night's sleep since before Butch was born. Nola, the doctor said I should begin to put my weight on my foot—cautiously, of course. So I can help you with the baby."

"I hate to give him back," Nola struggled with a waving fist that kept evading an armhole. "He's a darling rascal, yes, he is! Where I need help most is with the Colonel's Lady. Maggie seems to think I have two sets of arms and legs, the better to type her letters and run her errands. And she knows my days have two or three extra hours over the twenty-four." She yawned widely and handed Butch to his mother. "If you'll hold him, I'll get the coffee started. Then I'll poke him in his high chair."

When she had plugged in the percolator, Nola manipulated eggs and bacon, made toast, poured frozen orange juice into a pitcher and warmed the baby's cereal. Then she took Butch from his mother and strapped him into the high chair. Dottie came hobbling from the bedroom using the cane the dispensary had lent her.

When she had pushed Dottie's chair up to the table and brought coffee and food, Nola began spooning cereal into the baby. Sitting beside him, she looked out at the bright morning. The site of the quarters climbed a little toward the mesa so she could see the far reaches of the base across the hangars and landing strips. And suddenly her eyes filled with tears.

Dottie set down her coffee cup to say, "Push Butch's chair over here beside me. I can feed him so you won't have to drink your coffee in snatches—*Nola!* Honey, what it is?"

Nola wiped her eyes on a napkin. She ran the spoon around Butch's opening mouth and popped the collected cereal inside. "I was remembering how I fussed about getting up early to have breakfast with Tom. What I'd give to have him sitting across from me in our kitchen right now!"

"I know, I know."

"No, I don't think you do, Dottie. You don't have to feel guilty. You are a good wife to Jack, not a spoiled child-bride trying to get her own way in everything. Even to the time her husband would eat breakfast."

"It couldn't have been quite that bad."

"Yes, it could." Nola spooned more cereal into the baby's open mouth.

She wanted to tell Dottie all about it. How she had in a way tricked Tom into marriage, how Mama and Pa thought she was too young, too immature to think of being a wife. Maybe when Dottie heard it all, she might think Nola hadn't been all wrong— She pulled her thoughts up short. Foolish they were and immature they were on her part, but those quarrels were intimately hers and Tom's. She couldn't share them with Dottie in an attempt to justify herself.

She shook her head to clear the tears out of her eyes and reached again into the baby-food jar. "Come on, sweetie, grab this last bite. I must get to work." She gathered dishes into the sink and poured Dottie another cup of coffee. "I want to run home for a few minutes. Then I'll come back and take this youngun" —she paused to shake Butch's waving hand—"to the nursery."

The letter from Tom should be in her mailbox now. Mama would have sent it right on. Nola yearned for the letter and dreaded reading it at the same time. Suppose it said what she feared it might say? That Tom thought there was no use trying to keep their too-young marriage afloat? That he hadn't wanted to marry now and couldn't be bothered with the whims of an immature wife. That a soldier couldn't do his duty with part of his mind worrying at a personal problem. . . . Nola forced her attention back to Dottie.

She was saying, "Let me keep him here today. I can get around enough to manage. There will be plenty of time to put him in the nursery later, when I get some kind of job."

In her mind Nola could hear Pa's insistence that a girl must be able to earn a living. To a service wife some skill became imperative. The grim possibility that she would need it loomed large in wartime.

"Are you sure you can manage?" Nola looked into the refrigerator. "There's plenty here for lunch, and I brought in Butch's pants from the line last night."

"I want to write to Jack," Dottie said. "And I have some hems to do." She smiled at Nola. "Get on with you. There's sure to be mail in your box."

Nola drove back to her house dreading that letter all the way. Tom hadn't expected her to come back to Bitter Lake. Or he wouldn't have put the car in storage. The Colonel's Lady had known about that and had had the car sent around for Nola to use. Tom had plainly thought she would stay in the city, using one of Pa's cars. Tom had filled out a forward-card for the mail, cleaned out the refrigerator, even taken the

158

ivy plant over to Fran. He hadn't overlooked a thing, Nola thought fearfully, except the possibility that she would come home.

She used her key on the front door, walked through the rooms, dusted a few surfaces quickly, gave the retrieved ivy a drink, plumped the cushions that didn't need plumping. All to put off the moment when she must look into the mailbox and find Tom's letter.

It was there.

Nola turned it over in her hands. The writing was bold and decisive. Tom knew his own mind surely. The ink was black and heavy. Was that a symbol? She called on her courage and slit the envelope. With an unspoken prayer she began to read:

Dear Nola,

I wish I could talk to you tonight. I'm not so good at getting what I need to say down on paper, but I'll try. It would be so much easier to pick up the phone. You don't know how I long to hear your voice. But I know I wouldn't get said what I must. I guess I'm chicken. If I did phone, you could probably twist me around your finger the way you've done before.

And this time, my dear girl, I won't be twisted. I love you dearly and I want you to be happy. That's really selfish of me, for I am happiest when you are happy. I promised to love, honor, cherish and protect you and I will, no matter what hap-

159

pens. But I didn't promise to always agree with you.

Honey, couldn't you remember you made a promise to me, too? Maybe I don't need cherishing or protecting, even if I'd like them, but you couldn't truly love and honor me if I let you make my life over according to what you want at this minute. I know a lot of men do let their wives take full charge, and I'm damn close to doing it myself. I want to be with you and I can see just as plainly as you can that, if I came to the city and went to work for your Pa, you and I would be together more. There wouldn't be the long and frequent separations that the service will guarantee. But I would be less than a man if I let you persuade me to abandon the work that is honestly the most important thing in my life. Even more important to me than you are. . . .

Nola gasped and stopped reading right there. She wrung the pages together and furiously threw them into the wastebasket. To be told flatly that you weren't as important as flying a helicopter! Not as important as bolting a few sheets of plastic together to form a shield! Not as important as living in a remote hole that was "east of nothing, west of nowhere, and in the middle of trouble!"

But of their own volition Nola's hands stopped wringing themselves and retrieved the crumpled letter from the wastebasket. She smoothed the pages on her knee and read again:

. . . any abilities I may have are centered in my job. I can't let even you distract me from developing whatever talents I possess. And, honey, you shouldn't want me to be distracted. It wouldn't be self-sacrifice for me to give up my work and latch onto you; it would be self-indulgence. I would end up resenting the demands you made upon me.

So I'm not coming to the city just now for a visit, or later to stay for good. It would be for bad, anyway.

Remember me, Nola? I'm still the man you married. I hope I'm still the man you love. I haven't changed. I hope you'll see that you don't want me to change.

I hate to go off without seeing you, but that's part of soldiering too. Remember that I love you with all my heart and that I want you to be happy.

Yours always,

Tom

Standing in the middle of the painted rug, Nola read the letter again, this time without rage. She stood there for a long time holding the pages, staring at them unseeingly.

It was hopeless. She and Tom could never agree,

even if Tom wasn't convinced of that. He expected her to change, to plan their life together from his point of view. How could she if Tom wouldn't compromise? He would, though. Practicality told Nola Tom would give in on a few points if she did so. Then he might be edged away from a too-firm stand on other points. After all Tom's wife had had much practice in winding Pa around her fingers!

The phone startled her. She glanced at her watch in dismay. She was already half an hour late. The Colonel's Lady was doubtless at the temporary office they had set up for their project and would be sharp about Nola's tardiness.

When she picked up the phone, Mama's voice came over the wire. Why hadn't Nola called? What had happened? What was wrong? Had she received Tom's letter? Now there was another one. Mama would keep it until— What? Nola didn't mean to stay on in that dreadful place, did she? With Tom in Vietnam, what would keep her there?

Nola smoothed the crumpled pages of Tom's letter as she answered her mother's questions. She hadn't called sooner because she had been so very busy. Doing what? Didn't Mama remember the Colonel's Lady had a project going? If she had to shake the Pentagon to its foundations, that determined Maggie was going to get this soon-to-be deactivated base set up as a home for her wives and others like them.

They were calling it Dependents' Depot, and already

twenty wives had moved in, in addition to the wives already living in the quarters. Nola laughed a little. "Maggie figures if the wives get settled in, possession will be nine parts of the law. The Defense Department can hardly act like a hard-hearted landlord and throw the girls out. Look what that would do to their image!"

Everything was moving along quite well, Nola told Mama. But it took a lot of letters and persuasions to get such a project off the ground.

Yes, she had received Tom's first letter. It had come this morning. Please forward the other one too, and if more came—

"*No*, Mama," Nola heard herself saying briskly. "I'm not coming home right away."

Her mother's voice down the wire demanded, "What is there to keep you now that Tom has gone to Vietnam?"

"You've no idea how many irons we have in the fire," Nola said. "We want to get training classes set up for the wives and some recreation going. I'll start a drama club for the teen-agers. We have quite a few here, and it's important to keep them busy, so the wives without husbands don't have to cope with too many discipline problems. And the Colonel's Lady is pretty sure she can get a grant—in connection with the schools in Bitter Lake—to set up a training course for licensed vocational nurses. There's a secretarial course too. Maggie says those two courses are just a beginning, so you see I can't even think of coming home until we finish."

Pa spoke up from the extension then. "Nola? That is you talking? I want to be sure. For I can hardly believe my ears. Did I actually hear you say you had to *finish* something?"

thirteen ❧❧❧❧

JUST TELL ME

Nola kicked off her pumps. Poor feet, she had stood on them for twelve—no, thirteen—straight hours. Not for the first time she wondered what the Colonel's Lady was made of. After the umpteenth interview or patient explanation, she could go on to the umpteen-

and-oneth. Her hand in the velvet glove was iron, that Nola knew; the rest of her was probably tempered steel.

She yawned widely. They had lunched with the Better Business Bureau, met with the school board in the afternoon and dined with the Chamber of Commerce in town. "We'll need all the cooperation we can get," the Colonel's Lady had told the groups. She would get it too, Nola thought. Who could resist Maggie? Handsome and appealing, all she asked of anyone was their absolute best, so certain that she would get it that you couldn't think of disappointing her.

Dottie and Butch were asleep. Nola had planned to write to Tom before she went to bed too, but doubted now that she could stay awake long enough to finish a sentence. But the Colonel's Lady would lift an eyebrow if she didn't see a letter for Tom in the outgoing mail basket in the morning. She'd want to know why, and absolute exhaustion wouldn't be an acceptable excuse.

Finding a pen Nola sat in front of the sheets of paper but the words wouldn't come. "Darling Tom . . ."

Suddenly she wanted to be in the house that had been their first home. Dottie and Butch wouldn't miss her or need her for an hour or two. She would be closer to Tom there, closer to their love. In her own house, sitting at the table made from a packing case and skirted from an old evening dress, she could better write of the things that were in her heart.

She changed to slacks and sandals and tied her hair in a scarf. The wind tugged at the windows and swooped around the corners of the house. There would be sand blowing too. When she had first come, the constant wind had keyed her up until her nerves twanged, but now she didn't mind it. She could tell the newer comers that, after you got used to sand in your teeth, you found it was good clean dirt. It could be rearranged easily. Of course if you tried to get rid of it permanently, that was another story. The girls who adjusted found that if you dusted twice a day or if you didn't dust at all the results were the same. Then they relaxed and took up a hobby. The ones who couldn't live and let live as far as dust was concerned had nervous breakdowns and got divorces.

Walking down the road in the moonlight, she reviewed Tom's letter mentally. One thing he had written she remembered word for word. "I love you dearly and I want you to be happy. That's really selfish of me for I am happiest when you are happy. I promised to love, honor and cherish you, and I will, no matter what happens to me." She would repeat that to him. How could she better say what was in her heart?

She would tell him, too, about the busy days here at Dependents' Depot. That hasty name she had given would probably stick, no matter what formal and dignified christening came later. She might tell Tom, too, something that Pa wouldn't believe. That each of her former—and dropped—interests had opened up an opportunity here. She had nursed Dottie and cared for Butch using much that she had learned from the nursing course she hadn't finished. She had taught a variety of subjects although she wasn't a trained teacher. Whenever she or the Colonel's Lady had an idea and started another class, it had followed that Nola could pinch-hit until a better qualified and permanent replacement was found. She had modeled and danced, painted posters and the nursery playroom, started a bridge marathon and decorated the project office. At the moment she was swamped with enthusiastic teen-agers launched into dramatics. Maybe she would tell Pa. He might like to know that parents were always wrong!

But it would come hard to admit to Tom that he had been right. Mama and Pa were supposed to know best, but young husbands didn't necessarily have more answers than young wives. She would write how much she missed him, about how lonely she was. And to be sure he knew how much Tom Cartright's wife loved her husband she would tell him that several times.

Her house looked lonely in the moonlight, Nola thought. Maybe it missed her. Maybe a house shouldn't be left alone any more than a person. And it was only half alive when it was lived in by one person. A family was much better. Dottie had to keep going because of Butch, and he, with his baby delight-

168

fulness, made it easier for her to keep on in good spirits.

The shrubbery bent and swayed in the wind, making dark beckoning gestures that were repeated eerily by the shadows on the wall. A branch plucked at Nola's scarf as she went up the steps and the creak of the opening door made her shiver. As she turned on a lamp, something scuttled over the floor and disappeared among the protective colorings of the painted rug. It was only a spider, a small frightened one at that.

Nola sat at the table and pulled her chair up with a scraping sound that made her start. She busied herself with pen and stationery. As she had hoped, the words came easier here.

Darling Tom,

I am so glad to have your letter. I was so afraid you might not write to me. Why didn't you tell me you had to leave? I should have known you would go with the men you had been training but somehow I didn't.

Couldn't you talk to me more, Tom? About the things that are important to you? I'm ignorant about many things, but I want to learn. If you will just tell me—

She stopped to listen, holding her breath to hear better. Nothing more . . . Probably the outdoor equivalent of a small scared spider, she told herself, and went back to her letter.

—if I know what is expected of me, I'll do every single silly thing.

Strike out that word "silly." At first all the to-do about the right—and only—way to handle all the little social situations did seem silly to me, but I've learned there's a good reason for most of it so now I go by the rules. Stuff like the president of the organization or the guest of honor always pours at teatime, because that way everyone gets to see her and exchange a few words. So she must be ensconced behind the serving tray to hoist the coffee- and teapots.

And I've given up fighting with the Colonel's Lady, too. Bless her heart, she's going to educate me if it kills us both! You will be glad to know I get along with her real fine—

That was a footstep on the porch. Nola whirled with her heart in her throat. She hadn't locked the door. It began to open—

The Colonel's Lady looked almost as startled as Nola felt. She found her voice first.

"What in the world are you doing here, child? I saw the light and thought of a thousand things!" Whatever she had been holding inside her bag, she now let fall out of sight.

"I was too tired to go to sleep," Nola said defensively. "And I wanted to write to Tom."

"Why did you have to go walking in the middle of the night to write a letter? In an empty house!"

"It isn't exactly empty. I just don't live here for now. But I will again—"

"Will you, indeed?" Maggie Slayton's voice was soft, and Nola saw that she was smiling.

"Yes, I will! Indeed! I'm going to take full charge of my life and my conduct, and I'm going to do what I think best. I'm not going to be dependent on anyone to do things for me, or to tell me what I ought to do, or ought to think. Not even you!" Then hearing what she had said, Nola's hands flew up to hold her cheeks.

The Colonel's Lady was laughing now. She patted her hands lightly in a gesture of applause.

"I didn't mean that—" Nola stammered. Then she flung up her head. "Yes, I did mean it. What I didn't intend was to be rude."

Her visitor dismissed the rudeness with a wave of her hand. When she spoke, the words seemed irrelevant. "You haven't been late to work for several days, have you? And I haven't had to remind you of your schedule either."

"Oh, no," Nola said. "I'm so self-reliant, and self-controlled and self-disciplined that I make myself sick!"

"I diagnose that as a little self-pity," the Colonel's Lady said calmly. "I mustn't work you so hard."

Nola had remembered something. "I didn't hear a

171

car—" She opened the door and looked out at the road empty in the moonlight. "What do *you* mean going walking in the middle of the night?"

"I couldn't sleep either. Wes and I liked to take a walk at bedtime to look at the stars. So I still walk and wonder if he is looking at the same stars halfway around the world. Sentimental of me, isn't it? And the time wouldn't jibe either."

Nola thought of the Army wife in Honolulu. "A nice woman in Hawaii said that the longer you're married the more you feel the separations."

"It's absolutely true." Maggie Slayton looked down at her tightly held hands, her shoulders hunched against the inner cold of loneliness. "Each time is worse than the last time. You keep thinking that the luck has to run out."

Nola couldn't bear to look at her friend's face. But seeing the tear that fell on the clasped fingers was almost worse. She was on her knees before she knew it, holding the anguished hands in her own, looking up into Maggie's face with the empathy born of her own fears for Tom.

"Don't! Please don't, Maggie dear. Or I'll blubber until I'll have to take the day off tomorrow!"

The foolishly inadequate words, the first that had come to mind and tongue, made them both smile. The Colonel's Lady drew Nola into her arms, resting her cheek against the girl's hair, and so they remained for a long moment. The older woman released Nola then

172

with a sigh and a straightening of her own shoulders into the confidence she showed the world.

"No matter how much a good cry would help, we can't let anything prevent a regular fourteen-hour workday tomorrow," the Colonel's Lady said. "There's half a dozen of the wives to convince that they *want* to enroll in the LV nursing course set up in town. They'll need a car pool for it, too. And if that spotty face in the nursery is a case of chicken pox, we'll have to have an isolation ward."

Nola thought about it. "Could we put the kids in part of the men's ward at the hospital? With so many gone now, there won't be any pressing need for those beds. That way a few of us could take care of a bunch . . . if we can keep the kids in those big beds."

Maggie Slayton nodded and rose from the couch. "We have to play most things by ear, don't we? I'll go along home now. You won't believe how much better I feel after talking to you, Nola."

"But I didn't say anything."

"It isn't what you say. It's how I know you feel." She turned away. "But you didn't get your letter written."

"I was having a hard time with it. It's just about impossible for me to get what I want to say down on paper. I wish there were some way I could talk to Tom."

The Colonel's Lady turned back from the door, her competent self again. "There is a way. Come home with me and I'll show you."

They turned off lights and remembered to lock the door. Then they walked down the silent road toward the colonel's quarters in a companionable silence. Once Maggie Slayton said, "This is another good reason why the wives should be allowed to stay here. There will be guards, and we will be safe day and night. I hope you won't walk along at night any place else, Nola. I know I wouldn't."

In her house they went to the study where Maggie opened a drawer and brought out a small compact machine. She snapped in a tape pack and handed a microphone to Nola.

"Just push that button and talk to Tom until the tape runs through. Mail the tape to him tomorrow, and he can play it back for himself on a recorder Wes has with him. Or better still, we'll go to town tomorrow and buy you and Tom a pair of your own."

At the study door, she kissed Nola lightly. "Good night, my dear. I'm going to bed. When you finish, lock the door as you go out. And be sure to tell Tom that I say he's got a nice girl here."

Nola told Tom a great deal more than that.

Next morning she recruited three teen-aged candy-stripers who had had chicken pox, and together they turned an empty ward at the hospital into what Nola named The Chicken Pen. The first half dozen rashed and feverish patients were brought by their mothers

174

from home. The nursery phoned to report four others kept out because they were probably coming down. When the four were brought, Butch was among them, suddenly sick after Nola had left him earlier.

He whimpered and held out his arms to Nola. Instead of bouncing, he laid his head under her chin and sighed loudly.

"Don't feel so good, little man?" she murmured, cuddling him. "Let's go rock the baby."

She was leaving him asleep, damp and flushed of face, when a candystriper told her the Colonel's Lady was on the phone. "Nola, can you leave over there?" Maggie Slayton asked quietly. "Come over to the house, will you? I need you."

The receiver on the other end of the wire went down gently before Nola could say a word. The fear she lived with day and night exploded in her mind and shook her body brutally. *Tom* . . . it had to be something about Tom. . . . Dear God, dear God, don't let it be Tom—

Maggie Slayton met her at the door and, turning at once, led the way to the breakfast room. "I'm glad you could come, Nola. Sit down, please—" She gestured vaguely toward a chair. "I was just having my coffee—" She poured a second cup.

"Tom?" Nola's voice came out in an anguished whisper. "Maggie, *tell* me! Is it Tom? Is it?"

"No, no. Not Tom." The Colonel's Lady came round

175

the table to urge Nola into a chair. "Sit down, dear. Please do," she said in that strangely calm voice. "Tom is all right. He's all right."

"Then what *is* it?" In her anxiety Nola shook her friend's arm fiercely. "Tell me!"

"Tom has done a most heroic thing. A forward team was trapped by enemy fire when their helicopter was shot down deep in jungle territory," Maggie said. "The commander of the party"—she stopped talking, then resumed evenly—"covered the men's withdrawal until a rescue chopper arrived. Tom was piloting it. His shield protected the chopper from machine-gun fire until the nine-man team could get aboard. He could hover until the commander crawled back through a ring of fire that encircled them to bring in the other pilot, the one with the first chopper that had been shot down—"

"Tom wasn't wounded?" Nola could think of no one else. "Tell me, Maggie! Are you sure he wasn't hurt? Are you keeping something from me?"

Maggie Slayton sat very still. She shook her head. "It's just as I told you. Tom piloted the second helicopter. That shield of his made it possible to land under fire and pick up the others. He undoubtedly saved their lives."

The Colonel's Lady sat so still . . . controlled her voice so rigidly. Nola suddenly saw the anguish that her own anxiety had overridden. Her hands flew out to her friend.

"Oh, Maggie— The colonel. Was he—" *Don't* use the past tense, Nola told herself. "Is he all right?"

"Wes was the one who crawled through the fire to rescue the first pilot. They haven't told me how badly he was burned." For the first time Maggie's voice wavered. "He'll be flown back to a hospital stateside. Tom will probably bring him."

A flood of joy nearly drowned Nola. Tom was safe. He was coming home. *Safe . . . home . . .* home to her. It was indecent to be glad in the face of Maggie's dread.

She tried to hide her thankfulness, tried to say something helpful. "Since the colonel can be transferred, maybe his burns aren't too severe. Dear Maggie, I know you're worried to death—" Nola stopped aghast. "Why do I have to say that word!"

"Because we have to live with it. No, I'm not worried. All I can think or feel is thankfulness. Thankfulness that Wes will be out of it for a while," the Colonel's Lady said. "I should be ashamed to feel such relief, but it's the truth. He has been given back to me again."

She took a long breath and braced her slender shoulders. "But the reason I called you, Nola . . . I want you to come with me. We must go to Dottie. Jack was the pilot of that first chopper that was shot down . . . the one Wes pulled out of the fire. Jack died before they could get him back to the hospital."

fourteen 💕💕💕
NOW FOR NOLA

The Colonel's Lady tapped on the door, then entered without waiting. Dottie Harper stood in the middle of the room, rigid and silent, staring at the officer who had brought the news of her husband's death.

After a moment she seemed to swim upward from
178

the deep sea of her shock. In a level, unemotional voice she thanked the officer, saying that it must be hard to bring such a message. Closing the door behind him, she submitted patiently to the embraces and the clasping hands by which Nola and Maggie Slayton conveyed their sympathy and concern.

Nola found that you said whatever you could, never giving yourself time to think how totally inadequate words could be. Probably Dottie heard only the tone of their reaching out to her in love, felt the empathy that their clasped hands offered.

Surprisingly Dottie had heard more of what the officer said. She asked about the colonel's condition, spoke of his bravery in dragging Jack through the fire. "I hope it's a million-dollar wound," she said.

While Nola wondered if she had heard right, Dottie saw her bewilderment and explained: "A GI expression. A not-too-serious wound is worth a million because it takes you out of combat. Sends you back home or to the hospital where you're safe." Dottie's voice went flat. "I'm sorry I said that."

Although the words were spoken without direction, the Colonel's Lady answered, "Don't be. It's the truth. You said only what we are thinking. I can't deny that I'm giving thanks with every breath because my man is coming home. That thankfulness makes me understand your desolation even more, Dottie dear."

"I've always been afraid that people who are important to me will go away and never return," Dottie said. "When I was little, when Mama and Papa would quarrel and he went slamming out of the house, I'd never expect to see him again. Finally I didn't. . . . I'm always being left alone and I can't bear it . . . I can't. . . ."

"You aren't alone, dear." Maggie soothed the twisting hands and gently drew Dottie into the circle of her arms. "I won't tell you we know what the loss of Jack means to you, for we don't, but our love and compassion reach out to you. Nola and I and every sister woman on this base lift you up and sustain you with our thoughts and prayers. The saddest aloneness in the world is when no one cares about you. You can never be really alone again, Dottie, for many of us truly care about you."

Dottie's head rested on Maggie Slayton's shoulder, and her hands lay quietly in Maggie's clasp, but Nola doubted that she heard. Dottie had withdrawn into an inner desolation where shock mercifully numbed the reality of her loss. After a long silence she said conversationally that there was a fresh pound of coffee on the shelves. Perhaps they should make a potful. People would be coming in as soon as the word got around.

When Maggie had gone to the kitchen, Dottie thought of something else. She asked Nola, "Will you, let them know at the practical nursing class? One of the girls will let me read her notes, I imagine. I can arrange to make up the work later."

When Nola asked about notifying relatives, Dottie shook her head. Jack had no family at all, and she herself had only two distant cousins and a great aunt. Dottie thought they would be relieved, actually, not to know about the services until it was too late for them to come. But when Nola persisted, Dottie found her address book and pointed out the three names. "Thank you anyway," she said.

When the three short letters were written, Maggie Slayton brought in coffee. Dottie sat watching her cup grow cold. "Jack thought I made really good coffee," she said.

The words pulled out another small memory. Dottie smiled a little over her brittle words. "We never had any arguments over his mother's cooking either. She died some time before we were married but Jack remembered that she could ruin food faster and oftener than anyone he had ever known. He told me his mother said so herself."

Dottie set her cup down untasted and walked purposefully into her bedroom. They heard the squeak of the closet door, and the sound of drawers being opened and closed.

"If she would only break down and cry, wouldn't it be better?" Nola whispered. "Or should a doctor put her to bed? What on earth is she *doing* in there?"

"I imagine she is looking over her clothes," said the Colonel's Lady.

"Her clothes? *Now?*"

181

Maggie Slayton spread her hands in a small gesture. "To be sure she has something suitable for the funeral. If she doesn't keep busy, she will begin to think, poor child."

"What if I brought Butch home?" Nola asked, keeping her voice low. "He has some temp, and he's sure to be fretful enough to keep two or three people busy."

"A good idea," the Colonel's Lady agreed. "Go get him now. Be sure to wrap him up well on the way over."

A little later when Dottie took her flushed and blotchy little son from Nola, the tears finally came. As she wept, the Colonel's Lady gathered her and the baby back into her arms, her own cheek against Dottie's hair, Dottie's face hidden in the silky down on Butch's nape.

When the wives began to come with cakes and meat loaves, Dottie let Nola take the now sleeping baby into the bedroom. She stayed there with him until conscience drove her out. The Colonel's Lady was looking exhausted, and she needed some time with her own anxieties, Nola thought.

When Fran came, Nola persuaded Maggie to go home for a time to rest. Then she and Fran got Dottie to swallow the sedative the doctor had sent over. That accomplished, Nola organized a detail of wives to tend the door and the telephone. She got Dottie into the bedroom on the pretext of looking at Butch and once there persuaded her to lie down beside him until he went to sleep again.

"What will I do without you, Nola?" Dottie asked in a voice slurring with drowsiness. "Butch loves you until I'm almost jealous. And I depend upon you so much."

"What do you mean, 'do without me'? I'm not going anywhere."

"You said you couldn't stand it here, that you wanted to go live in the city where your family is. That was before Tom went, even."

"I said a lot of things," Nola admitted. "I'm not too crazy about military life but I've decided—" Nola had meant to say "the only important thing is to be with Tom" but it would be cruel to remind Dottie of her own loss with such words. So she hastily substituted: "—to show Pa and Mama and maybe Tom that I'm really good for something. No matter how the Colonel's Lady works me to death, I'll stick it out with Dependents' Depot. To the end. Bitter or not."

"I never wanted to be anywhere except with Jack," Dottie's voice caressed the name. "It may be different with you. You have your family."

"I remember your parents at the senior party in high school, I think."

"They broke up right after I graduated. Dad went away, and three weeks later he was killed in a car wreck. Mama just didn't get over it. Two months later she went too. By the sleeping-pill route."

183

"Oh, Dottie, I didn't know—"

"How could you? It might have taken me longer to believe they'd rather be dead than with me, but I had to go to work. I'd wanted to be a nurse but that was out. They needed civilian clerks at the air base and I got on. That's where Jack and I met."

Nola tried to think of something to say, but what was there to say? She settled lamely on, "Hush now, honey, and try to get some rest."

"Why? So I can look fresh for Jack's funeral?"

But the bitter voice was also drowsy, and in a few minutes Dottie had drifted off to sleep.

Then there was nothing to do but wait for Jack's body to arrive, for Tom and Colonel Slayton to come. In the desert of time there was one small brightness. The Colonel's burns were painful but not severe. He could come home, then check into hospital a day or two after the funeral.

A surprise came on the weekend. Great Aunt Clara arrived with enough luggage to last until the plans she had for Dottie and Butch could be put into effect.

Gray-haired, talkative and brisk as an east wind, Great Aunt helped Nola move back into her own house. "Naturally, I will take care of Dottie and dear little John now. You will want to get ready for your husband's homecoming."

Aunt Clara proposed changes for her niece. "Your mother was always my favorite, Dottie, though I did
184

want to starch her backbone a little. She just couldn't cope with trouble, poor youngun. Nobody let me know what happened to her and your father. When I did find out, you were already married, so I've just sat back and minded my own business. But now you need me and I need you. I've got this big old house that's close to one of the finest nursing schools in the country, and because I like crazy kids, I always take a few students. So you can come stay with me and be a nurse like you've always wanted, Dottie. And I'll spoil little John."

She waltzed the laughing baby around the room telling him, "If he's a good boy, he can come live with his Gr'aunty and chase her cat and climb trees and grow up to be a credit to his folks!"

Nola said in an undertone to Dottie, "I thought you said she was old!"

"I heard that, young woman," Aunt Clara said. "I may be old but I'm not decrepit, thank the Lord. Don't you know when a woman makes it to sixty-five, she can go on forever? Run along now, Nola. I'll wash these dishes and then put these two down for an early night. Dottie's going to take a pill and get some rest." Aunt Clara tickled the baby and dropped him into his high chair. On the way past she cupped Dottie's face in her hands and bent to kiss her. "These are hard days for you, dearie, but we'll get through them."

As Nola started for the door, Aunt Clara called to her. "Honey, will you see if you can get the food turned off? I know the girls love to do something for Dottie but we've got enough now to feed Coxey's Army—" She interrupted herself. "Do you know who Coxey was? Or why he needed an army? I've said that all my life and never thought before to look it up. Well, see you tomorrow, dear."

At home, Nola smiled as she straightened and dusted. How wonderful that Dottie had someone to lean on, someone who cared greatly. Wholesome and nourishing as home-baked bread, Aunt Clara would be a broad and willing buffer between Dottie and more adversity. Dottie wouldn't stop grieving for Jack, but she could go on living in the belief that hope lay beyond despair. Who could despair around Aunt Clara?

At the airport late next day, a kind of shyness kept Nola at the back of the crowd. When she saw Tom . . . when he saw her, there would be time to rush forward. For the same reason she had driven there alone. Before she left the house, the phone had rung several times but she had not answered it. She didn't want to wait at the airport with Maggie Slayton and be a third when husband and wife met, any more than she wanted her meeting with Tom under her friend's eyes, no matter how friendly the gaze would be.

The plane swooped to the runway, the honor guard and the pallbearers came to attention. The colonel emerged bandaged and moving stiffly. Nola kept her gaze hungrily on the doorway. Tom would come any minute.

But he didn't. The coffin was removed and taken away between the ranks of the guard. The colonel finished his duties and went off with his Margaret. Nola shrank back out of sight so they wouldn't discover her. When Fran's surprised eyes caught her in a doorway, Nola almost ran back to the parking area.

She sat for a moment before starting the car, the blaze of sun turning the tears in her eyes to a mist of diamonds. Tom wasn't on the plane. He hadn't wanted to come home to her. Her change of heart hadn't come soon enough. She wasn't to have the longed-for second chance.

Back in the little house she began packing. As she moved clothes out of closets and drawers into her luggage, she tried to shut her mind to thought. If you meant to keep going, you couldn't give yourself time to think. The Colonel's Lady had said that when death came to Dottie's heart and house. As death had come here . . . the death of love . . . the death of marriage. . . .

The phone rang loudly in the silent house. Nola looked at it but didn't pick up the receiver. It wouldn't be Dottie, not with her husband's body resting under the flag in the post chapel. It wouldn't be the Colonel's Lady, not this soon. She hadn't had time to realize that her man was home again. It might be Fran, curious about Nola's retreat from the airport. And surely, it wouldn't be Tom.

When the phone stopped ringing, Nola called the airport in town for a reservation. As she waited for the clerk's reply, she remembered that the plane going to the city left only a few minutes before the plane from the city landed. That was the kind of irrelevant fact you put through your head to keep from real thinking.

After her case was closed, she cleaned out the refrigerator. She stood a moment holding a pound of butter and the package of steak she had brought in dry ice from the city. How short a time since she had come so eagerly for a reunion with Tom, to find he had gone back to the war. Fran and Dick could eat the steak and Aunt Clara might find room for the butter in Dottie's crammed storage. But Nola put the packages back into the freezer. Surely Tom would be back sometime to the little house that had been their first and only home . . . after he was sure she was out of the way. She rubbed her cold hands together in a vain attempt to warm them.

In town she drove first to the garage where Tom had stored the car and left it again in storage. Then she taxied to the airport, picked up her ticket, checked her luggage and walked toward the starting gate. The wait would be short.

As she passed through the wide corridor, Nola stared without interest at the display cases of clothes
188

from specialty shops, the paintings and maps on the walls, read the posters on the bulletin boards. Her name leaped to her attention.

Teen Theater announces the opening of "Two's Company; Three's Triangle" on Friday and Saturday nights in the Rec Room at Bitter Lake Base . . . written by . . . the cast includes . . . directed by Mrs. Tom Cartright. . . .

Nola thought it would be a miracle if Jerry got his lines up by opening night. If she could have heard him through the sides a few more times. Carol's dress wasn't right either. If the belt were raised it might be better. And the blocking in the first act—
She stood staring unseeingly at the bulletin board. She didn't hear the flight being called, she didn't notice the emplaning passengers eddying around her. Without some help Jerry wouldn't get up his lines, Carol's dress would remain wrong, maybe the Teen Theater couldn't even go on with the play without Mrs. Tom Cartright, director.

With her friend gone so suddenly, Dottie might plunge back into despairing certainty that the people she loved would always leave her, never to return. With no one to attend to the multiplying details of the project, the Colonel's Lady wouldn't feel free to go with her husband when he had to enter the hospital. In fact, thought Nola with her usual self-confidence, if Maggie had to rummage through all the details she hadn't handled before, she might miss something crucial to the whole housing plan. For want of a Nola, Dependents' Depot might be lost.

"Look, *you!*" Nola told herself, fiercely and aloud. "You aren't walking out on all these commitments! You hear me? You're going back to the base to finish every blasted one!"

The first two passengers deplaning from the city flight heard and stared curiously. Then they moved around her and went on. The third passenger stopped abruptly, then swung on his heel to come to her. Tall and tanned and even thinner, Tom's eyes were soft with love and longing as he caught her in his arms.

Nola stood there for a blessed moment leaning her forehead against his chest. Then she stepped back and looked up into his face. It was a time for putting into words all the love that overflowed her heart, all her resolution to be the best of all possible wives, all her gratitude for the second chance.

Instead Nola heard herself saying, "My clothes have flown off to the city!"

"What clothes? Where?"

"I thought you weren't coming home. Didn't you get any of my letters?"

"The chopper bringing up the mail crashed and burned. What do you mean you thought I wasn't coming home? I left the colonel at Phoenix to fly to the city and bring *you* home. I wish you'd stay put, Nola!"

How brief the moment that had been her reprieve! If she had boarded that plane that had now flown away with her luggage, she would have missed Tom by minutes. If she had walked out on the kids at the Teen Theater, on the housing project and the Colonel's Lady, on Dottie who would need her help to get through the hard time of Jack's funeral, it would have meant she had gained none of the maturity and responsibility she needed to make a good marriage. She would have lost the second chance to prove to Tom that the flickering fire of being in love had grown to a strong steady flame . . . enough to warm their hearts, their home and their lives.

It won't be perfect, Nola warned herself. How could it be when she was so far from perfection! The lack of security, the separations, the loneliness of a soldier's wife couldn't tip the balance when being together lay in the other scale. "Whatever needs doing, I'll do with all my heart," Nola promised humbly.

"No one is going to stay more put than I," she told Tom. "From now on. I'm going to be very busy"— with laughter that was a salute to Pa and the Colonel's Lady, she went on—"finishing things! And making you into the kind of husband I deserve!"

Tom laughed and held her close to his side as they moved away from the stream of passengers.